The Perfume of Lust

The Perfume of Lust

by
Gaston Danville

Translated, annotated and introduced by
Brian Stableford

A Black Coat Press Book

ISBN 978-1-61227-580-2. First Printing. December 2016. Published by Black Coat Press, an imprint of Hollywood Comics.com, LLC, P.O. Box 17270, Encino, CA 91416. All rights reserved. Except for review purposes, no part of this book may be reproduced or transmitted in any form or by any means, electronic or mechanical, including photocopying, recording, or by any information storage and retrieval system, without permission in writing from the publisher. The stories and characters depicted in this novel are entirely fictional. Printed in the United States of America.

Introduction

Le Parfum de volupté by Gaston Danville, here translated as *The Perfume of Lust*, was first published in 1905 by the Societé du Mercure de France. It was the author's last novel, although it was probably not intended to be; the list of works included in the preliminary material announces another book "*en preparation*" entitled *Kakemonos*. A Kakemono is a Japanese scroll intended to be hung on a wall, containing a picture or writing, so the projected text might have been a work of nonfiction rather than fiction, but all we know for sure is that it never appeared. We also know, from the dates of composition included at the end of the text, that the publication of *Le Parfum de volupté* was somewhat belated, presumably indicating the author's difficulty in obtaining publication.

Danville's three previous novels had appeared initially as serials in the *Mercure de France*, a periodical with which he was closely associated, but this one did not, although it did appear from the press associated with the magazine, perhaps by way of a reluctant concession. With one distinctly anomalous exception, however—a propagandistic war story published in 1916—he did not publish any further fiction there, or anywhere else. The publication of *Le Parfum de volupté* does not seem, therefore, to have been an encouraging experience, and the book is now exceedingly rare, so it presumably sold poorly. It is however, a remarkable novel, groundbreaking in several ways—perhaps too innovative and enterprising for its own good, in the context of its day, although its extraordinary qualities are perhaps easier to appreciate today.

"Gaston Danville" was the pseudonym of Armand Blocq (1870-1933), the younger brother of the neuro-physiologist Paul Blocq (1860-1896), a colleague of Jean-Martin Charcot at the Salpêtrière hospital. Danville was one of the principal collaborators involved with the early issues of the *Mercure de France*, founded in 1890 by Remy de Gourmont, Alfred Vallette and others to provide a voice for the burgeoning Symbolist Movement. The *Mercure* was not the only periodical that attempted to do that, but it was by far the most successful, and it survived long after the movement in question had lost its crusading zeal and Symbolism had melted into the general cultural background, eventually being over-taken as a contender for the literary *avant garde* by its more exotic descendant, Surrealism.

At the time of the *Mercure*'s foundation, the Parisian literary scene was replete with disputes between various literary "schools" and "movements," of which Symbolism was one of the most prominent; it had developed out of Romanticism, once seen as revolutionary in its reaction against Classicism, but long lapsed into a kind of orthodoxy. The term "Symbolism" was closely associated, in the contexts of those disputes, with "Decadence," a label once resolutely adopted by some of the more radical Romantics, after having initially been leveled at the movement as a term of abuse by the critic Desiré Nisard, and resurrected in the 1880s as an assertive banner. Symbolism was widely seen as being engaged in a crucial rivalry with Naturalism, which was considered by many commentators to have recently evolved from its origins in the work of Émile Zola and the Goncourt brothers into a "neo-Naturalist" phase represented by "psychologists" such as Paul Bourget, who placed more emphasis on the literary examination of internal states of mind than external behavior in their accounts of the human predicament.

The apparent opposition between Symbolism and Naturalism was illusory, mostly a phantom of publicity, and had much to do with the fact that the Symbolist school was primarily a school of poetry, crucially associated with avant-gardist poets, such as Stéphane Mallarmé and Jean Moréas, whereas Naturalism was primarily a school of prose fiction, closely associated with the evolution of the narrative techniques of the novel. Naturalist novels did not shun the employment of symbolism as a narrative device; nor did Symbolist writers, when they diversified into prose fiction, shun the devices developed by novelists in the interests of representational verisimilitude. Leading writers of both schools shared a keen interest in the seamier side of social life, and were routinely preoccupied with erotic and violent subject-matter. Nevertheless, many of the individuals caught up in the controversy did see themselves as being involved in an ideological conflict of sorts, and were sometimes eager to take up positions in the front line, firing their critical weapons with reckless abandon. Gaston Danville was one of those, but he was exceptional in the particular stance he took, and the location from which he elected to campaign. He was, in a sense, the most ideologically-extreme of all the neo-Naturalists, but he took up his position at the very heart of the Symbolist movement, as a cuckoo in its most precious nest.

Alfred Vallette became the editor of the new *Mercure*, and his wife Marguerite, who had already become famous under the pseudonym of Rachilde, became one of its most frequent early contributors, along with

Gourmont, Jules Renard and Saint-Pol Roux, all of whom would have identified themselves unhesitatingly as devoted Symbolists. To begin with, essays and reviews took up the bulk of its pages, mapping out the field of Symbolist literature and art and promoting its virtues; and while the page-count remained at its initial figure of 32, priority was given to poetry with regard to creative material. Once the number of pages had been doubled to 64 at the beginning of 1891, however, prose fiction was able to play a more important parallel role in carrying forward the ideals of the movement.

Much of the *Mercure*'s early prose fiction was very brief, in the tradition of the "prose poetry" that had been launched forty years earlier by Aloysius Bertrand and Charles Baudelaire and subsequently hailed by Joris-Karl Huysmans as "the osmazome of literature." The fictional contributions to the magazine made in its first few years by Gourmont, Saint-Pol Roux and Renard all belonged to that lapidary tradition, and many of the other contributors followed suit, although, when Vallette was able to increase the page-count again, to 96 in 1893 and 128 in 1895, he was progressively able to find room for longer works, including serial novels—and when its periodicity eventually increased from monthly to fortnightly in 1905, those serial novels, in accordance with continuing changes in literary fashion, became a far more important feature. From the very beginning, however, Remy de Gourmont was interested in expanding the scope of prose-poetry beyond the merely lyrical, and adding more substance to it. In that quest, Gaston Danville must have seemed to Gourmont and Vallette to be an ally; his early contributions to the magazine resemble standard exercises in Symbolist prose-poetry, and the series he began to develop from them, collectively entitled "Contes d'Au-Delà" [Tales of the Beyond], seemed a natural development in terms of the elaboration of their narrative method and concern.

Vallette would have found out soon enough that Danville did not consider himself to be a Symbolist at all, but he obviously did not consider that to be a reason to exclude him from the periodical, the scope of which he was probably ambitious to broaden from the very start—and which did, indeed, ultimately become a magazine of general literary interest, as the Symbolist crusade in which cause it had been launched increasingly came to resemble a fad, and somewhat passé. At any rate, although Danville was never to appear as prolifically again as he did in 1891-2, he remained a regular contributor for more than thirty years.

In 1891-92 Danville published twelve "Contes d'Au-Delà" (all translated in the Borgo Press collection *The Anatomy of Love and Murder: Psychoanalytic Fantasies*) in the *Mercure*, plus two other prose-poems that did not appear under the rubric but can nevertheless be considered offshoots of the sequence; those items were reprinted in volume form by the periodical's press, with some additional material, in 1892. In 1893 Danville published a longer story in the *Mercure*, which did not bear the same series title but is an obvious extrapolation of the same line of endeavor, and he published a further item of the same sort in 1894. After that, however, he changed direction markedly.

Danville's first four novels—*Les Infinis de la chair* [The Infinity of the Flesh] (1892), *Vers la mort* [Toward Death] (1897), *Les Reflets du miroir* [The Reflections in the Mirror] (1897) and *L'Amour magicien* [Love the Magician] (1902) all carry forward the same project that he had begun in the "Contes d'Au-Delà," as he explicitly

9

stated in the preface to the first of them, which explained the theory behind the story series and advanced the claim that it would attempt to take the Naturalist cause to a new but logical extreme. The essay also identifies Symbolist and Decadent literature, in contrast to the various subspecies of Naturalism, as "degenerate." The essay is dated 1 November 1892 and is, therefore, contemporary with Max Nordau's scathing attack on *fin-de-siècle* "degeneracy," *Entartung* (1892; tr. as *Degeneration*), which Danville could not have read before offering his own thesis, although he might well have had some inkling of Nordau's argument; Nordau wrote the book in Paris and had a very strong interest in contemporary psychology, so he might have been acquainted with the Blocq brothers.

Vallette, who must have read that preface, although *Les Infinis de la chair* was published by Alphonse Lemerre, evidently did not take offence at the description of Symbolism as an essentially degenerate form of literature, but it probably did not endear Danville to some of his fellow contributors to the *Mercure*—even those who, like Remy de Gourmont, were perfectly willing to consider the adjective "decadent" as a compliment. Danville's novels do not appear to have enjoyed much success, however, and such celebrity as he still retains is almost entirely based on his non-fiction book *La Psychologie de l'amour* [The Psychology of Love] (1903), which went through numerous editions and was still in print when he died. He also wrote two other non-fiction books dealing with psychological issues, *Magnétisme et spiritisme* (1908) and *Le Mystère psychique* [The Mystery of Mind] (1915).

La Psychologie de l'amour was contemporary with Remy de Gourmont's *Physique de l'amour: Essai sur l'instinct sexuel* (tr. as *The Natural Philosophy of Love*), which was published by the *Mercure*'s press in the same year, and makes an interesting comparison with Danville's book. Danville's "Contes d'Au-Delà" were composed and published alongside some of the stories that Gourmont subsequently collected in *Histoires magiques* (1894; tr. in *Angels of Perversity*) and both series are illuminated by a comparison that suggests a certain mutual influence. They must surely have discussed their parallel non-fiction projects, and their relevance to the fiction they were writing.

Danville was by no means the only litterateur active in the *fin de siècle* period to take a strong interest in parallel developments in psychological science, and the entire neo-Naturalist school, whose analyses of human behavior had progressed from the hereditary theses of Émile Zola's Rougon-Macquart series to the quasi-psychoanalytical theses developed with great fashionability and considerable commercial success by Paul Bourget, was more-or-less compelled to keep an sharp eye on its developments. On a more popular level, the rapid evolution of crime fiction had also taken aboard a powerful fascination with theories of criminal psychology. In Danville's view, however, the neo-Naturalists and writers of popular crime fiction were somewhat behind the times, routinely clinging, tacitly or explicitly, to scientific theses he considered to be obsolete. He wanted to take his place within—or perhaps to constitute in its entirety—a new *avant garde*, producing literary works explicitly based in up-to-date psychological theory. By virtue of that very fact, however, his plans brought the method and substance of his work into close association with some key Symbolist endeavors.

Because of its nature, Symbolist literature was intensely interested in fantastic material, and a good deal of Symbolist fiction is explicitly supernatural. The fact the Symbolist writers were operating in an age when supernatural notions had all-but-lost the warrant of belief, however—which is why Danville, in 1892, considered such traffic "decadent" or "retrogressive"—meant that such motifs were very rarely represented as simple matters of fact; indeed, the whole point was that they were *symbols*, ideas essentially representative of something else, and not mere accidents of happenstance. For the Symbolists, the apparently-supernatural was really the psychological, reflective of internal emotions and obsessions. Exactly the same was true for the Naturalists, the principal difference being that the Naturalists were usually explicit in declaring the seemingly-supernatural to be delusory or hallucinatory, while the Symbolists, not considering that to be a crucial issue, routinely left the ambiguity unsettled, allowing the images to speak for themselves. The effect of that distinction was, however, weakened—in Gaston Danville's work more than most—by the fact that Naturalistic narratives adopting the viewpoint of a deluded or hallucinating character are compelled to represent their delusions or hallucinations as *apparently* real.

The invocation of the supernatural in Symbolist prose fiction is much more obvious in short fiction than novels, and there is an obvious correlation between the length of Symbolist prose works and their usage of natural representation and narrative development. This is not surprising—indeed, it is inevitable, given the innate naturalism of the narrative techniques typical of the novel—and it is arguable that there is really no such thing as a Symbolist novel, the principal candidates for that designation being distinctly patchy, either because of their episodic quality (as, for instance, in Gustave Kahn's *Le Conte de l'or et silence*, tr. as *The Tale of Gold and Silence*)[1] or because that they carefully embed significant Symbolist interludes in thoroughly naturalistic narratives (as, for instance, in André Beaunier's *L'Homme qui a perdu son moi*; tr. as *The Man Who Lost Himself*). That pattern is very obvious in Gourmont's work, and equally obvious in Danville's, nowhere more so than in *Le Parfum de volupté*, which surely warrants consideration as a semi-Symbolist novel shored up with the aid of Naturalist techniques.

Many of Remy de Gourmont's short stories are "contes d'au-delà" in the perfectly straightforward and commonly-understood sense that they are blithely supernatural, even when their supernatural motifs are obviously symbolic of erotic urges. Many, therefore, consist of brief Gothic fantasies, either horror stories of the *conte cruel* variety or delicate dream-fantasies in a more sentimental vein. Danville's choice of "Contes d'Au-Delà" as a title for his own series was, however, consciously and determinedly ironic. The "Beyond" from which his tales come is the unconscious sector of the mind. Danville's characters are haunted, but they are haunted by urges that they cannot consciously comprehend, and the poignant emotions and memories provoked by those secret spurs. All their apparitions are delusory, and although that does not prevent them from seeming real to the deluded protagonists, in exactly the same way that the symbolic devices in Gourmont's stories seem real to his characters, the underlying rhetoric of their presentation is essentially different.

---

[1] Black Coat Press, ISBN 978-1-61227-063-0.

The fact that Danville was insistent in basing his accounts of delusion and obsession on what he took to be sound theories of positivistic psychology did not, of course, prevent him from writing horror stories or delicate erotic fantasies; indeed, it is arguable that it added an extra dimension of cruelty to his *contes cruels* and an extra dose of intensity to his eroticism. Although Gourmont, like Danville, was fascinated by the manner in which erotic impulses occasionally led to suicide and homicide, Danville's interest in delving into the psychology of suicide and murder was more intently focused than Gourmont's. In the same way, when Danville went on interest himself in possible transformations of the way in which the human mind might deal with erotic impulses originating in the unconscious, as he does in *Le Parfum de volupté*, he did so in a fashion that aspired to be more detached and clinical than Gourmont. Danville approached the substance of erotic impulsiveness not to indulge in it, let alone celebrate it, but to inspect it from without—from a kind of beyond where few litterateurs attempted to assume a stance.

In theoretical terms, inevitably, Danville's work was unable to be any more sophisticated than the prevailing ideas of its era, and the psychologists on whose work it is principally based—primarily Théodule Ribot,[2]

---

[2] Théodule Ribot (1839-1916) was one of the great pioneers of "positivist" psychology, explicitly based on the philosophy of Auguste Comte, which eliminated from consideration all the nonmaterial attributes associated with the "spiritualist" school, whose notion of the soul had been philosophically revamped by Descartes, attempting instead to formulate an entirely physical notion of mentality. When Danville wrote his early fiction

of whom Paul Blocq was a dedicated disciple—have long since fallen out of fashion. Danville's early fiction is therefore likely to seem primitive to the modern reader in its use of the terminology of "hysteria" and its development of such recently-hatched notions as that of the "doubling" of the personality, but his short stories were genuinely experimental in their day, not merely in their supposed scientific basis but their situation in the forefront of the literary *avant garde* of their era. The relative coolness of his contemporary reception does not mean that the work in question was of no innate interest, and its unique features still recommend it for the attention it did not receive at the time.

The explicit connection that Danville tried to forge between literary endeavor and psychological science had been tacit since their origins and had inevitably become more obvious over time. The notion that literary depictions of human psychology, especially its more exotic manifestations, constitute a kind of research and analysis that can and ought to be considered a kind of *avant garde* of the science, perhaps far ahead of it in sophistication, had been proposed long before the 1890s, and the argument was viable long before the advent of the novel, perhaps extending all the way back to Homer. What was original about Danville was not so much his literary ambition but his conviction that literature had recently lost its lead in the quest to generate understanding of human

---

and essays, Ribot had not yet published his two books most relevant to their arguments, *L'Évolution des idées genérales* (1897; tr. as *The Evolution of General Ideas*) and *Essai sur l'imagination créatrice* (1900; tr. as *Essay on the Creative Imagination*), but Danville would undoubtedly have read both before completing *Le Parfum de volupté*.

behavior and mentality, by virtue of maintaining overdue allegiance to obsolete models of motivation and the mind. Perhaps he had too much faith in the potential of contemporary psychology to correct that flaw, but he was surely not mistaken in his conviction that the literature of the future could and would benefit from further development of its scientific sophistication, especially in the artistry of its dealing with the human Beyond of the unconscious.

In the preface to *Les Infinis de la chair* Danville represents his fiction as an aspect of an endeavor whose parallel non-fictional development had already commenced in an article entitled "L'Amour est-il un état pathologique" [Is Love a Pathological State?], which was scheduled to appear in the *Revue philosophique* (edited by Théodule Ribot) and was subsequently published in the February 1893 issue of the periodical. In effect, it constitutes a preliminary sketch of *La Psychologie de l'Amour*. The argument it presents is detailed and elaborate, drawing on evolutionary theory (Darwin and Schopenhauer are cited) and literary evidence (including works by Paul Bourget and Benjamin Constant) as well as numerous treatises in psychology, attempting to fuse those various threads into a coherent whole.

Danville's article eventually refuses to conclude that amorous attraction is a kind of mental abnormality—more specifically, that it is a symptom of "degeneration"—in spite of its often obsessive character, as Jules Hosch had done in his remarkable collection of literary studies in psychology *Folles amours* (1878).[3] The fact

---

[3] The author in question, by then spelling his surname Hoche, published a speculative fantasy developing his own ideas about that theme in the same year as *Le Parfum de volupté*: *Le*

that the possibility is considered so earnestly is, however, revealing, and the story-lines of Danville's novels, whose amorous heroes are all deeply troubled—the protagonists of *Les Infinis de la chair* and *Vers la Mort* both end up committing suicide—have the opposite implication. *Le Parfum de volupté* does not suggest that amour ought to be reckoned a form of mental illness either, but it certainly suggests, forcefully, that a better and more life-enhancing kind of sanity might be possible in that regard, if only humans had the mental capacity to develop it.

In the context of his account of *La Psychologie de l'Amour*, the most interesting of Danville's first triptych of novels is *Les Reflets du miroir*, which is an explicit extrapolation of the theory of amorous attraction set out therein. That novel had had a preliminary sketch of sorts in the novelette "Mousmé" (1893), which is far more graphic in its hallucinatory imagery, and in its development of the symbolism of dreams. The inclusions of hallucinatory fantasy in *L'Amour magicien* are more elaborate, and although they are conscientious their development of Scandinavian mythology, they too reflect a strong interest in the potential symbolism of dreams. *La Parfum de volupté* can be seen as a logical development of that burgeoning interest, although it takes a further step in the direction of typical Symbolist artifice in maintaining an unusually convoluted ambiguity in treating the question of whether Robert Toby's account of his experiences is hallucinatory or not.

Faiseur d'hommes et sa formule (1905; tr. as *The Maker of Men and His Formula*, a volume that also includes translations of three stories from *Folles amours*; Black Coat Press, ISBN 9768-1-61227-426-3..

It is arguable that Danville's short fiction was more interesting than his early novels, partly because their necessary economy freed them from the tangled verbosity and ponderousness that often sometimes him when he wrote at greater length, but partly, too, because they did retain, in spite of the author's convictions and rhetorical thrust, a strong Symbolist influence. The best of them retain a pungent hint of Remy de Gourmont, and it is difficult to avoid the suspicion that although Armand Blocq was consciously a positivist and a neo-Naturalist, "Gaston Danville" was always, perhaps unconsciously, a Symbolist, far more fearful of intimate hauntings than any true positivist would ever admit to being. *Le Parfum de volupté* seems to confirm that suspicion, in a striking fashion.

Le Parfum de Volupté clings to Naturalist conventions by virtue of the multiple devices used to put narrative distance between the reader and the main story, related third-hand with abundant commentary conscientiously endorsing the notion that the whole experience might have been a hallucination, while pointing out, equally conscientiously, its extraordinary detail and coherency. In addition, it rationalizes all its fantastic devices as elements of the lost science of ancient Atlantis, thus shifting the text out of the realm of supernatural fiction and into that of *roman scientifique*. The real interest of the novel, however, for the reader and writer alike, is not the literary apparatus simultaneously supporting and undermining the supposed plausibility of Robert Toby's story, but it's psychological implications: its argument regarding the psychological roots of "volupté" (which is usually translated as "sensuality," for euphemistic reasons that I considered inapt as well as unnecessary in the present instance).

Within the tradition of *roman scientifique*, *Le Parfum de volupté* is closely connected with a particular strand that had made significant progress in recent years, that of speculative accounts of hypothetical societies in which sex is liberated from the legal and moral constraints to which is was subject in contemporary French society, which had come to seem to many people to be intrinsically absurd and a source of a great deal of unhappiness. Whether writers of the period were sympathetic to it or not, the notion of "free love" popularized by the thriving political theories of Anarchism was a challenge that all designers of literary utopias were virtually compelled to address, especially as Joseph Dejacque's archetypal account of *L'Humanisphere* (the fictional component of which is translated as "The Future World (of the Humanisphere)"), first published in the late 1850s but long banned in France, had finally become readily available thanks to an 1899 reprint published in Brussels.

Danville had probably read Paul Adam's *Lettres de Malaisie* (1898; tr. as "Letters from Malaisie"),[4] although he evidently finished writing *Le Parfum de volupté* before having had a chance to read André Couvreur's *Caresco, surhomme* (1904; tr. as *Caresco, Superman*),[5] which beat it into print and might perhaps have made it seem a trifle tame and tentative when it followed in its wake. Danville must also have completed his novel before reading another classic *roman scientifique* focusing on problems of amour, *Le Surmâle* (1902), by Remy de Gourmont's friend Alfred Jarry,

---

[4] Also included in *The Humanisphere*, Black Coat Press, ISBN 978-1-61227-511-6.
[5] Black Coat Press, ISBN 978-1-61227-254-2.

which is similarly more forthright, but Danville's novel clearly belongs to the same cluster of works and owes its genesis to the same imaginative ambience. It might also be worth noting that *Le Parfum de volupté* was probably published in the year which Han Ryner actually wrote his Atlantis-set utopia *Les Pacifiques* (tr. as "The Pacifists")[6] although the latter was even longer-delayed in publication, not reaching print until 1914.

All of the stories cited offer different views of how the concept of "free love" ought to be construed, and what the sociological consequences would be of establishing some such institution—or absence of institution—on a general scale. No synthesis of the conflicting opinions was ever achieved, nor was it ever likely to be, but it is perhaps odder that the question soon faded back into the realm of the unasked, even though none of the social and psychological problems associated with the slowly-shifting *status quo* seemed to show the slightest trace of amelioration. At any rate, Gaston Danville's approach to the problem, although far more tentative and coy than those of most of his contemporaries, is remarkable in proposing that the problems posed by the psychology and sociology of amour might be soluble—and, more importantly, might *only* be soluble—by means of a fundamental mental shift altering the essential anatomy of thought.

Obviously, the story cannot offer a very detailed account of what that shift would constitute; as the characters discussing the matter point out, the terminology is lacking because contemporary vocabulary is shaped by the attitudes that have been transformed, but it is never-

[6] Included in *The Human Ant*, Black Coat Press, ISBN 978-1-61227-323-5.

theless ingenious in dropping hints and planting sign-posts, using as a facilitating device the eponymous hypo-thetical psychotropic scent. Although it is arguable that the author takes polite discretion a little too far—the novel contains what is surely the only orgy scene ever described in which none of the participants actually touches any of the others; the veils carefully drawn over all the physical contacts that can be presumed to take place are remarkable in their censorious abundance; and the author has recourse to asterisks in the only sentence in which Robert Toby actually refers to the sexual or-gans—but that only helps to make the central obsession of the narrative seem more vividly awkward, as the au-thor clearly felt it to be.

Indeed, it is possible that the reason that Gaston Danville effectively gave up writing fiction after pub-lishing *Le Parfum de volupté*, abandoning the literary quest that he had defined and propagandized in the in-troduction to his first novel, is perhaps because he simp-ly found it too difficult and uncomfortable to carry for-ward in the context of his own very obvious inhibitions. If that is the case, then his final effort can also be con-sidered as an interesting exercise in seething frustration as well as a fascinating study in hypothetical erotic psy-chology. Either way, of course, it offers a blatant invita-tion to symbolic decoding, in the context of the emergent schools of psychoanalysis pioneered by Sigmund Freud, of which Armand Blocq, as an ostensible positivist, could not possibly have approved. One is tempted to think that if Danville had been familiar with the Freudi-an theory of dream-symbolism, he would surely never have penned the final scene of his melodramatic plot—but perhaps he was, and knew exactly what he was doing. Sensitive readers will doubtless be able to make up their own minds.

This translation was made from a copy of the 1905 edition of the novel kindly loaned to me by Marc Madouraud; I am very grateful to him for allowing me access to an exceedingly rare and interesting text.

Brian Stableford

THE PERFUME OF LUST

I. The Smoking-Room of the City of Rio

This is the story that was told to me aboard the *City of Rio*,[7] in the course of a voyage from San Francisco to Hong Kong, by Vincent Tricard, a representative of the Maison Loupe, of Bordeaux (mustard, gherkins, etc.)

He told me that he got it direct from Toby—Robert Toby—himself.

It is, therefore, as you can see, a second-hand story.

As much for that reason as because of various accessory details—which will be revealed in due course—and the quality of the individual (as for Toby, I've never met him), I'm unable to estimate the measure of veracity that the story might contain.

Tricard was a likeable fellow, a dark-haired southerner with an easy-going manner, whose nature easily linked me to his acquaintance. In any case, on the Amer-

---

[7] The S.S. *City of Rio de Janeiro* was a real ship, launched in 1878 and acquired by P.M.S. in 1881, which travelled regularly between San Francisco and Hong Kong with ports of call in Honolulu and Yokohama. Danville records that he began writing the present novel in 1900 in Honolulu, perhaps during a stopover in a voyage made in the ship in question. He would not have known then, but would certainly have known by the time he finished writing the novel in 1902, that the *City of Rio* sank in February 1901 when it struck a reef outside San Francisco Bay; 135 people perished in the disaster.

ican boat, we were the only Frenchmen aboard, except for one second-class passenger, a cook who was going to Honolulu.

Knowing the steamers of most of the navigation companies by name, Vincent Tricard excelled in the comparison of their merits and faults, their speed and their respective comfort. He had, I think, traveled to all the lands, black, red, yellow and white, where mustard is consumed. Thus, he abounded in anecdotes, reeling off memories with the same facility as samples, a precious traveling companion not only because his chatter was a distraction, but also because of his real knowledge of the peoples and customs of numerous countries.

Of the multiple adventures whose incidents he re-traced for me, with a more intense interest in developing the heroic or comical side of them than retaining them within the bounds of plausibility, the most extraordinary was that of Robert Toby; that is why I shall try to tran-scribe it here.

I only obtained the full details little by little, for in this instance, contrary to the manner he usually adopted toward me, Tricard showed himself, at least to begin with, exceptionally reserved. However, I don't think the chronological order of his confidences is of any im-portance, and I shall take no account of it subsequently.

The first time that Tricard broached the subject was on the second or third day after our departure from San Francisco, because I remember that after "tiffin" the "boys" began to install the punkahs of which the dining-room ceiling had been denuded until then.

As the heat was increasing, we had not watched the Chinese working for very long and had gone up on deck, hoping to find a little freshness. But there, under the rear canopies, the temperature was unbearable; the sun was overheating the thick canvas and was doubled by a terrible reverberation. The sea, a harsh blue, was reminiscent of a recently-cast metal sheet. There was no breeze. A few Americans were lying on *chaises longues*, quite indecently, without jackets or waistcoats, their congested faces damp with sweat. The last detail took away any desire to imitate them.

There remained the foredeck.

Now, the ships of the P.M.S. Steamship Company are particularly sought out by Chinese passengers in steerage, because the company guarantees that in case of decease during the crossing they will not be immersed; furthermore, they always repatriate a considerable number in their coffins, which takes up room. So, they are often obliged to moor a part of the cargo along the forward bulwarks, in such a way that only a narrow corridor remains between the merchandise and the fittings of the spardeck—a corridor that one finds, as often as not, invaded by a host of Celestials, these living, heaped up almost everywhere, some lying on mats and others crouching down, playing with their bicolored dominoes.

That was the way it was that afternoon: heaps of galvanized iron juxtaposed with pieces of wood, crates of vegetables and boxes in which melancholy horses, devoid of an appetite, were huffing into their troughs, scattering wisps of hay and roundels of sliced carrot. As for the Chinese, they were, as usual, occupying the rest of the available space.

The scant air furnished by the velocity of the vessel was thus fouled by various emanations, and there was no means of attempting to take a walk, in the course of which one would have tripped over the fellows at every stride, who didn't budge unless one stepped on top of them.

Fortunately, having arrived at the smoking-room, we discovered that, in spite of it exiguity, it remained an agreeable little corner, fully exposed to the wind, and which, with all the windows open, and with "long drinks" in front of us, ice and cigarettes, we would have felt quite comfortable—I could even say completely comfortable—if it hadn't been for the continual racket of the Chinese players whose shrill and screeching voices hadn't been resonating incessantly like the chatter of a flock of magpies.

In spite of that inconvenience, sometimes augmented by gusts of complex odors when the boat yawed, the place remained possible, and Vincent Tricard and I were to return there frequently at that hour, the hour of the siesta. It was, in any case, much too hot for it to be reasonably feasible to sleep. The other passengers judged the matter differently, to which we owed being rarely disturbed. Sometimes, however, a few gentlemen from the Far West, in shirt-sleeves, came to sprawl on a banquette, in order to start snoring conscientiously, joined toward evening by others of their kind, who generally started a poker game.

Perhaps those circumstances contributed to urging my companion further and further forward along the road of confidences, which began as follows.

Once the smoking-room had been discovered, Vincent Tricard sat facing me in one of the swiveling armchairs with a fixed pivot sealed at the tables. We were alone. He began by smoking, talking about insignificant things—the weather, among others.

"More comforting than the mists in the region of Newfoundland, eh, this Pacific sun?" he said. "I've never got used to that filthy fog."

"Yes," I replied. "The deck drowned in a dense vapor that masks the masts and the sea, the calls every minutes, the 'eyes'—the two men in waxed garments, somber and immobile statues suddenly looming up near the prow, permanently sounding the surrounding opacity—and every lurch seeming like an effort of the enormous vessel to get away, while the trepidations of the pistons and the propeller, the heavy noise of the engines, which never slow down, warn you that a thousand human lives are being launched at top speed into the unknown, perhaps gliding toward another monster as invisible to us as we are to it. Yes, that spectacle has all that could be desired to procure the most blasé individuals a frisson that leaves an impression, at least the first time."

"Evidently," he said, "but for me, it's combined with another impression."

"A…mental influence? A special nervous reaction?"

"An influence…a special reaction, if you wish…a strange influence, even."

The face of the representative of the Maison Loupe, of Bordeaux, had darkened. Usually jovial and loquacious he fell silent after those last words and no longer seemed to by any more preoccupied by my presence thereafter than that of Bobbie, the captain's dog, a black and white rat-catcher incessantly on the hunt, ferreting right and left, which passed between our legs at that moment. For my part, not unduly concerned to know what appeared to have impressed Vincent Tricard so lugubriously, I respected his silence, and, as Bobbie had gone on to other tasks I looked out of the little window at the trajectories of the flying fish that were skimming the crests of the waves, silvery gliders scintillating in the sunlight, to transform themselves at the end of their course into heavy black stone birds swallowed up by the water. One might have thought that every turn of the propeller chased them from the flanks of the ship like flocks of frightened swallows.

A quarter of an hour went by, only filled with the sounds of the ship and the ocean, low-pitched sounds dominating the cries of the Chinese around us, the clink of coins and dropped dominoes.

Then Vincent Tricard got up, rang for the boy and, when the latter arrived, ordered two Manhattans.

As soon as the liquor had been poured over the ice piled in the glasses, he drank his in a single draught, and began:

"You must have found me bizarre, no? Oh, don't protest—me, who generally doesn't engender melancholy... It's always the same; every time I think about it, I...and I've reflected, you see; it's better to confide it to someone."

"Believe that I don't..."

He didn't allow me to continue. "It's decided! To think that for ten years—that's a long time, isn't it?— I've been keeping it to myself... Well, no; it'll end up choking me. After all..."

He didn't finish the sentence he'd started, but went on: "You don't understand? I must seem more and more idiotic."

"But..."

"Wait! That cocktail has done me good. Permit me to have a second before telling you...the thing."

II. The Red Fog and Leaden Toby

Where were we?

Oh yes, the fog!

That's the thing: it's better, in fact, to go back to the beginning, and the beginning dates back, as I told you, about ten years, perhaps even a little more...or a little less...I no longer remember, exactly.

I only remember that we were five travelers— commercial travelers, that is—four Frenchmen and a Belgian, on the *Normannia*, a German steamer of the Hamburg-New York line, built in England, which has had adventures since.[8] It became Spanish during the Cuban war and I think it ended up under the French flag of the Transatlantique.

Naturally, we all had places at the same table, and we were always together, because at that time, as the ships didn't yet stop over in Cherbourg, there weren't many passengers speaking our language, and it was an astonishing hazard that brought five of us together there. I was content with that, of course, but later, damn it, I'd rather have been alone all the time with no many how many sauerkraut-munchers, instead of...

---

[8] The *S.S. Normannia*, built in Glasgow and owned by the Hamburg America line, was hit be a tidal wave in January 1894 while traveling from New York to Algiers, and was indeed subsequently purchased by the Spanish Navy in 1898 for use in the Spanish-American War, before passing to the Compagnie Générale Transatlantique in 1899 as part of a debt payment. It was still in service when the present novel was published, but was scrapped in 1906.

Enough!

There was Choupot, who must now be associated with a *compradore*[9] somewhere out there in China; Filette, the Belgian, who's died since of fever in the Congo; Moizeau, who's still on the move; and the famous Bob, who was our doyen: Toby, Robert Toby. You must know his name: Toby, the sole survivor of the wreck of the *Dauphiné*?

Oh, the wreck of the *Dauphiné*...! If anyone had ever told me that I'd know what I know. Let's go! I'll continue, because otherwise I'll get embroiled in all the details of that damned story, and you see, it's necessary that I tell it once and for all, that I rid myself of it...yes, rid myself of it entirely.

You mustn't think that five cheery fellows like us were bored aboard the *Normannia*. Every evening, there was champagne, spirits and hands of manille, and mote rounds of spirits, until, toward eleven o'clock, sometimes quarter past, we were thrown out of the bar...when I say the bar, I'm mistaken; there was no bar there, it was the smoking-room—nearly eight times as big as this one—which served as a bar.

One night, as we were coming out, the fog arrived all of a sudden, so quickly that no one had time to cry out. Oof! A dirty fog in which one couldn't even see the forward lamps—it's necessary to say that the smoking-room was placed in the middle of the boat—and we hadn't taken two steps on the deck than a pitch capsized

---

[9] A comprador or compradore, was an indigenous manager—female in this case—of a European business establishment in South-East Asia. The term means "buyer," and compradors were responsible for purchasing local goods to be loaded on to ships for transportation to Europe.

all five of us. Oh, no great damage done, and besides which, I think we were a little tipsy.

Then the siren stated to howl.

You know what that's like, eh?

I don't like that noise, to be sure, but it never produced such an effect on me before.

Then I said: "I know someone who won't be sleeping in his cabin tonight—me."

The others writhed with laughter, except for Bob, who said: "Hey, if you're going down to fetch a blanket, fetch mine up too. I'll stay with you."

"Good night, brave lads!" The others were joking, you understand. But it didn't make me go to bed— definitely not! Why? I've often asked myself that, since.

When I came back up with my plaid, Toby's, and a flask of rum that I'd brought to keep the damp at bay, what do I see? My Bob, who, instead of having chosen, from the heap of chairs moored for the night, what we needed to lie down tranquilly between the funnels, sheltered from the wind, is standing up, clinging to the rail, in spite of the fog, the spray and a damnable north-westerly breeze that whipped your face!

I shouted to him: "Have you gone mad, Toby?"

"Go and see the point!" he replied.

"Eh?"

"Well, what?" he was speaking very calmly, in a funny voice. "I asked you to go and see the point."

The point is pinned up at midday; you know that as well as I do, so you can judge the effect that the question had on me, posed at that hour, especially in the tone he'd taken.

I think: *Right! There's a chap who's had too much to drink and can't hold his liquor.* I look at him. *He doesn't seem drunk at all, the clown!*

He didn't turn round, standing very straight, staring at the line in the water where the light stops before the mist, not seeming to care about the pitching or the rolling, and the *Normannia* was pitching terribly. Every time, she dipped her nose in the ink, one couldn't see the prow steeped in foam because of the mist, but one could sense it going down, I can assure you.

I reflected again: *Perhaps I ought to go down to my bunk after all...*

I gave up on that: the blasts of the siren were cutting through me, you could hear them everywhere.

I don't know what was the matter with me.

Is it because I was a bit tipsy, and that one can get ideas when one's drunk? I felt that I couldn't stay in my cabin with that diabolical music! I resigned myself, unavoidably, thinking: *Bah! What does it cost me to flatter his mania? If he's a bit drunk or a bit crazy, too bad! I don't want to sleep down below. I don't want to!*

I advance toward Toby, though, and try to reason with him.

"You're not thinking, old man. Where do you expect me to find the point? The smoking-room's closed now."

"Go to the glass in the first-class companionladder."

I was tempted to reply, *if you want it as much as that, go yourself,* but, I repeat, I was already troubled by the champagne, the spirits, the fog and the blasts of the siren, and his voice, which didn't seem to me to be natural, ended up taking away what remained of my common sense.

I could only see one thing, which was that I didn't want to sleep down below, and in truth, since it was necessary to stay on the deck, I thought I might as well pander the Bob's whim. Then again, his presence reassured me. One isn't proud at moments like that.

I clung on to the hand-rail, and nearly fell down the stairs several times, but I finally brought the point back to Toby.

"Now can we go to bed?"

Well, I hear him murmuring something like: "425…425…that gives seventeen and a half...seventeen knots and a half…It's almost midnight. If we haven't had too much difficulty maintaining that speed in the fog, *we're getting close…*"

I hear the last phrase and, giving up on convincing him, and also feeling, given that I'm shivering every minute when the siren starts moaning again, the need to have someone nearby, I stick myself against him and I ask him: "We're *getting close* to what?"

He shrugs his shoulders.

Surely, I ought to have left him there, not persisting, but no. There are times when one's stubborn. I shouted at him: "Come on, Bob, explain yourself!"

In reality I was beginning not to feel very well. Leaning over the side, the lights that were filing over the water were dazing me, and I sometimes thought I could make out the forms of giant icebergs advancing toward us—that was the fog.

More quietly, I said: "Are you talking about reefs?"

He continued to remain silent.

Then, crazy ideas passed through my mind. What did Toby mean by that? There was no land visible... A reef…? Impossible! The place where the *Dauphiné* had been wrecked…?

Then there was the stupid fear, the plain, baseless fear that nothing justifies, the fear that grips you by the throat and stops the blood in your veins. I drank my flask of rum in large gulps, and when it was empty, I threw the flask overboard. I didn't hear it fall, the wind and the waves were making such a terrible din.

The alcohol immediately lit me up like a punch-bowl in my head. The flames began to spin like suns in the midst of the waves, growing and spitting out sparks, and in its turn, the fog caught fire. Yes, the fog turned red and began undulating to the left and the right, following the rolling of the boat, and from back to front, according to the pitching.

Toby didn't move, but he seemed to me to be very big and very heavy.

I thought: *Soon, this is going to end badly! That red fog is going to set fire to the ship, or Bob, who's made of lead, will become so heavy that we'll sink...*

The ideas a man has when he's drunk, eh?

But the worst thing was when my fear came back...and I had no more rum! Toby continued to grow, or rather to weigh more heavily on the deck, which was at times down to sea level—as for that, that might be true, because the wind had freshened a lot—so much that I could see, at those times, the fire descending above us into the funnels, threatening the gangway, and then the foam washed through the scuppers.

Then I shouted to Toby: "Say something! You can see that what you can't tell me is weighing on you, weighing too heavily! Lighten yourself...go, on, lighten yourself..."

He didn't understand the craziness that was pushing me, of course, but he took my words figuratively, as a manner of speaking, didn't he? A figure of speech! No, it wasn't one, and I know—I'm an honest man, Monsieur!—that if I hadn't spoken, I was holding my knife open in my pocket, in order to empty him of what was weighing him down so heavily...what was weighing him down too much...

Although, as I've already said, the worthy Vincent Tricard, representative of the Maison Loupe, of Bordeaux, was a southerner by birth and temperament, and hence inclined to dress up the most banal adventures with a dramatic quality, I have never doubted the confession that escaped his lips then, for I suppose that the force inciting him, reluctantly, to confidences resided in that painful memory.

What was "choking" him, the thing of which he wanted finally to "rid himself," was, I think, the memory of that homicidal intention, soiling his career as "an honest man." That exaggeration of a metaphor, which, in the daze of drunkenness, had brought him to imagine that a similar burden of memories risked dragging his friend and the *Normannia* into the same disaster, that amplification of an image, must have engraved itself unwittingly in his soul, and had pursued him with an incessant remorse until the liberating moment when, with the aid of the cocktails and the gin, he had relieved himself.

And indeed, immediately after the instant when his clenched fist, punctuating it by thumping the table, on which the crystal of the glasses quivered, had confirmed the disturbance of his narrative, Vincent Tricard fell silent. The fellow's bronzed face had cast off the mask of ferocity and crime that had for a few seconds, transformed the visage of the placid traveler into the face of a bandit. Again, sitting facing me, was a tranquil sales representative, a slightly vulgar traveling companion, and I was already resigned to never knowing the famous Robert Toby's extraordinary story.

It is, in fact, probable that that disinterest would have deprived me of the continuation of that strange adventure if Tricard had not subsequently, on multiple occasions, taken care to revive my weakening curiosity, to sharpen it, by employing in the course of our conversations numerous allusions to Bob, his journeys, and above all the mysterious point attached to his shipwreck.

Robert Toby thus became a fantastic and troubling being, whose name irritated me, at the same time as my desire increased to be informed as to the deeds of that individual, who gradually took on the proportions of a legendary hero in my mind. But the more precise my attempts in that direction became, the more Vincent Tricard's reserve was augmented; he opposed a defiant mutism to my discreet questions. Perhaps he was reproaching himself for having said too much.

It was therefore necessary for me to employ cunning and patience to persuade Tricard to unveil for me what he was dissimulating with so much care, and I only extracted his secret in fragments, obtained with difficulty, at irregular intervals.

The most that he granted me, and which permitted me to connect certain morsels together that had been previously incoherent and sparse, was not in the little smoking-room of the *City of Rio*; it happened one evening in Honolulu, a port of call where a shortage of coal caused us to lay over for two days, and where, having perceived that my traveling companion talked more willingly under the influence of alcohol, I had ignobly got him drunk in a noxious "saloon bar," his divagations only having for witnesses a few gentlemen of color perched on high stools and accompanied by "flower girls" who understood as little French as their companions. Then, another time, one night in Kyoto, he told me the rest.

III. The Dauphiné Goes Astray

Toby had, therefore, spoken—and had thus escaped a danger as real as any of those he had braved in his numerous voyages.

He had even—the first step leads to a second and one can often go a long way in that manner—spoken all through that interminable night of fog and tempest, and doubtless for long days afterwards, perhaps because the extraordinary aspect of Toby's revelations had at first necessitated fear and drunkenness in order for them to provide in Tricard a complaisant, attentive and credulous listener; and then the pleasure, for Toby, of finally telling someone who listened without contradicting him or stopping him had sufficed, along with Tricard's awakened interest.

He spoke, and Tricard leaned that the place to which they were "getting close"—it was for the verification of that fact that Robert Toby had sent him to seek the point at such an unexpected hour—was the place where the *Dauphiné*'s adventure had commenced.

Then, Toby had continued.

One Friday evening, the *Dauphiné* had quit the port of Le Havre, taking with her three hundred emigrants, Italians for the most part, a hundred cabin passengers and her hundred and sixty-five crewmen. She was a Transatlantique of between five and six thousand tons, which, like all those of that line in that epoch, took ten days to complete the crossing to New York.

She had never arrived there.

After three weeks of waiting, as she did not appear off Long Island, it was decided to send steamers to search for her, but no ship, steamer or sailing ship, had sighted her. Although no wreckage had been found, the steamer was added to the list of lost ships in the Bureau Veritas.

Much later, Robert Toby was fished out of the water, half-dead with fever and exhaustion, alone in a waterlogged dinghy, deprived of rigging and food. It was a Norwegian three-master that picked him up, in the middle of the Gulf Stream, a long way from the American coast, and no one was ever able to render an account of how that might have happened, at least two months after the presumed date of the wreck of the *Dauphiné*.

In what fashion had the man lived in the meantime?

Why had he remained the only survivor of his six hundred companions?

No response was obtained to these questions, because Robert Toby, once embarked aboard the *Hulda*, delirious, was disembarked in America, where he was treated as insane, in an asylum, and when he emerged therefrom to return to France, after two years of internment, people were occupied with other things than the wreck of the *Dauphiné*. Cold showers, bromides and electricity had, moreover, taught Toby respect for the truth—which it is in fact, indecent to display nakedly.

Between the curt mention in the Bureau Veritas and the rescue of Robert Toby, therefore, the unknown extended: a very mysterious unknown. It was to be the privilege of Vincent Tricard, and then me, to some extent, to know what that terrain concealed, florid until then with hypotheses and appropriately planted with plausibilities.

Naturally, it has been impossible for me, as will easily be understood, to discern whether Toby's unhealthy visions and Vincent Tricard's drunkenness had been susceptible to distorting, enriching or diminishing its contents. Thus, I shall limit myself to doing my best to expose the facts, with the least possible commentary, and with the impartiality that is the duty of a conscientious historian.

According to Robert Toby, as recounted by Tricard, when the *Dauphiné*, after a few days of peaceful navigation, arrived in the vicinity of Newfoundland, without the preliminary condition of the sky and the earth permitting any anticipation, she was subjected in the course of a spring afternoon, to a series of terrible assaults.

Enormous waves raced from the depths of the horizon.

The passengers were immediately sent to their various locales, all the openings were blocked and all the hatches sealed. Those defensive preparations had scarcely concluded when the ship suddenly reared up before a frightful mountain of surging water. At the first contact, an icy avalanche descended, washing away the majority of the dinghies and one of the two large lifeboats, and carrying off the bridge, its machinery, and the officers and crewmen of the watch. Then, while the masts broke, there was a descent into a glaucous liquid precipice, the madness of the engine, the propeller spinning in the void; one of the piston-rods snapped.

The second wave plunged into the funnels, extinguishing the fires, with such a din that they believed that everything was exploding and that the vessel was about to sink. Stokers were scalded by jets of vapor. In their hold, the emigrants, seized by panic, tried to break down the doors and get out at any coast. There were stampedes, howls, women stifled, children trampled, knives plunged into the backs of men who nevertheless remained upright, so intense was the rush toward the exits, agglomerating the crowd in a compact block of tremulous flesh.

When that wave had passed, no living being remained on the deck, and water was streaming through the disemboweled lounge, inundating the interior corridors, where dementia was beginning to reign.

The rudder, torn away, was battering the rear, threatening to stave it in.

The last swell that agitated the boat with a formidable shock was more benign, being content to strip the deck of the masts and all the scattered rigging that encumbered it, shaking the mass of the dented, twisted vacillating funnels and carrying away the rudder.

Fortunately, the sky retained a consolatory serenity; the atmosphere, momentarily disturbed, was no longer troubled even by a faint breeze, and the sea had recovered such a calm that one might have thought that the *Dauphiné* was still moored in the harbor at Le Havre. And as, although weighed down by the water she had taken aboard, silently, with her fires extinct and her engine mute, no longer steerable, deprived of her captain, first lieutenant, helmsmen and deck-hands, laden with dead and wounded, the transatlantic liner, now defying the turbulence, was still victoriously afloat on the placid ocean, the panic that had taken possession of all the souls on board gradually calmed down.

The surviving officers reassured everyone.

In a few hours, the boilers would be functioning again. While a spare part was fitted to replace the broken piston-rod, the auxiliary engines would be employed to pump out the water. With the aid of the emigrants they would establish an improvised rudder rapidly enough. The breach in the deck would be repaired. There was, in any case, three months' supply of food in the bunkers.

The zeal of the crew, in combination with everyone's good will, would facilitate the accomplishment by the general staff of a task that was certainly not easy, but was sure now of being brought to a successful conclusion.

In brief, everything that the officers could say in such a circumstance, they said, and the Italians returned to their hold cheerfully, while the passengers lingered on the devastated deck, which the sun rendered less lugubrious, thinking that they had had a lucky escape.

But the three lieutenants, the pilot, the six engineering officers, and even the physician, the steward and his deputy, knew full well that the affair was not terminated, but that, on the contrary, the struggle was only beginning—and in what conditions! They knew that a ship without a captain, without a compass or a rudder, could no longer be called anything but a wreck, and that they would remain at the mercy of the eternal enemy that had just laid them low with a treacherous blow for a time they could not estimate.

How could they avoid a collision, if they ran into fog?

By what means could they ward of a definitive catastrophe if the barometer fell, and if the bad weather so frequent in those parts descended upon the poor crippled vessel?

And above all, how could they stop drifting? From that night on they would be carried far away from the busy routes where their sole chance remained of finding a helpful comrade that could offer to take them in tow.

Save for the steward and the chief engineer, the remainder of the general staff consisted of young men—brave, it goes without saying, but how much is courage worth before such responsibilities? And even though, without weakening, without losing a minute, they had put everyone to work, prodigal with words of hope, more than one held back tears of rage on thinking secretly that they were terribly impotent to offer effective protection to the human lives of which they had taken charge.

But there was a miracle!

They had good weather for two weeks.

A few days after the accident, the dead had been properly buried at sea, with a flag for a shroud and their feet weighed down with lead. The wounded were reposing cozily in unoccupied cabins, the infirmary having been too small. In well-organized shifts, the emigrants and the sailors shared the work, day and night. The spardeck had been more-or-less patched up, where the first-class passengers, newly admitted thereto, remained pensive before the rude traces that the sea had left in its passage.

They studied the davits, empty of boats, save at the rear, where three boats had resisted, and the remains of the cast-iron colonnettes that had supported the bridge. Then they reassured themselves, before the urgency with which hammers were brandished over red-hot metal, illuminating the anvil, and the planes guided along planks. The forges roared, the chains of improvised lifting-tackle grated in the midst of commands to "Hoist!" and "Lower!" the rumble of steam in the windlasses, short and robust, which their position on the upper deck had protected, and which never ceased extracting new equipment, wood and iron from the bunkers...

A joyous activity filled the inert mass of the steamer with noise. The recent drama, the deaths and the damage were forgotten. Confidence overflowed in cheerful appeals, songs and laughter.

The spardeck, however, being entirely bare except for the funnels, offered a singular appearance. No mariner, officer or sailor, could have seen the stumps of the masts, now carefully sawn off, sticking up, the balustrade with its new rails, their white paint scarcely dry, without reconstructing in thought all the rigging, from the shrouds to the highest yardarms, above which the flags had floated, high in the wind, on the day of departure, searching instinctively for the silhouettes of the men on watch on the bridge, the commander's cap, and, on finding instead of that a strange construction-site dirtied by coal, chippings and sawdust, experiencing a new sadness every time.

While the repairs were being carried out, the *Dauphiné*, in conformity with the dictum claiming that the deviation is worth as much as the route, drew further and further away from the course that she would normally have followed. Slowly, she drifted southwards. The point was always taken at midday, as usual, and the little flags marked the position of the ship, descending thirty miles, and even fifty miles, without provoking anything but optimistic reflections among the passengers.

"That direction is equivalent to an insurance against tempests..."

"A northward drift would have exposed us to fogs..."

"Maintaining a straight line, we would have risked collisions..."

And a thousand appreciations of that sort, among which returned, like a chorus: "Bah! As soon as the rudder's set up, we'll soon have made up the lost time!"

The rudder!

When the monstrous piece was finished, laid out on a bed of beams, freshly tarred, barded with metal and as shiny as one could wish, no one doubted that ill-fortune would henceforth be entirely repelled, so much did that solid, shiny, brand new mass emanate an impression of strength that constrained confidence and hope.

At lunch, the first-class passengers had champagne sent up, and toasts were drunk to the officers, the crew and the brave Italian workers.

In the evening, a celebration was organized, in the course of which pretty American collectors amassed a considerable sum of money, which was to be divided on arrival between the mariners and the emigrants.

After two fruitless attempts, which exhausted the men and their leaders, the enthusiasm diminished. Few people aboard were able to react against such a disappointment. Women lamented. Many Italian women threw themselves to their knees, frantically embracing their crying children, and invoked the Madonna, weeping, as if misfortune were imminent and a catastrophe had become inevitable. People conversed in low voices. Men with pale faces talked to the emigrants about a revolt.

"If we have to stay like this, broken down in the middle of the Ocean, facing the prospect of certain death, at least, before dying, one has the satisfaction of doing justice to the incapable, and since the provisions heaped up in the hold are no longer of any use except to nourish the fishes, let's employ the little time we have left in feasting and carousing!"

Elsewhere, the most absurd proposals were exchanged and seriously discussed:

"Could we not steer the ship some other way? By means of lateral rudders, for example, easier to fit? Why persist in trying to reestablish that heavy piece that's cluttering up the deck, demanding that it by set in the traditional place, at the risk of damaging the rear during the operation, of breaking the propellers and killing the workers? Since it's proven that the means at our disposal remain insufficient, which ought to have been easy to foresee, it's madness to persist in wanting to do everything correctly, in accordance with the maritime art..."

"In that case, there'd have been as much value in trying to recreated the destroyed masts and fittings..."

"One can recognize there the spirit of routine typical of mariners...and while those messieurs are persisting stubbornly, in vain, who knows what dangers we're running?"

Others affirmed that, from the first day, it would have been better to detach one of the remaining boats.

"The best of the boats could have been chosen; if necessary, it could have been fitted with an improvised deck, and, amply furnished with foods, it could have gone to seek help. Then, by now, it's not at all improbable that we'd have already been taken in tow by a steamer sent to search for us..."

They cited examples, and, taking their hypotheses for realities, became indignant, with grand gestures, disdainful expressions, animated and furious faces.

But the majority did not listen to the speechmakers, the angry and the critical. They did not hide their depression, and only found relief from their sadness by expanding themselves in a flow of childish plaints:

"It's necessary to expect anything."

What use were those recriminations, and what was the point of inventing futile expedients? The state of the vessel, a lamentable pontoon, was sufficient indication that no hope of deliverance was permitted to its prisoners. No sail had been perceived since the accident. Although the weather had favored the repair of the damage, tomorrow might bring another cyclone, which would render it futile. The two checks suffered in the placing of the rudder seemed like two warnings. Would it not have been better to perish right away, like those who were now at rest in the bosom of the waves, rather than agonizing slowly like this…?

Twenty-four hours went by: hours of insults and tears, fever and anguish; dolorous hours in the course of which the energy of the officers themselves was often close to failure, submerged by that crop of murmurs and plaints.

The third attempt, recommenced after the day of rest granted to the crews, finally succeeded.

One of the servo-mechanisms of the tiller had been carried away with everything else, but a second subsisted at the rear.

Everything was finally ready.

The following day, in the afternoon, the boilers were put under pressure again.

Then, to the acclamations of all, amid the applause of the passengers, the happy delirium, the cries of joy and the songs of the emigrants, the second lieutenant, who had become the commandant, having given the course to the helmsman, shouted in a voice strangled with emotion the banal: "Forward, slow!"

And again, the giant heart of the engines beat, slowly at first, and then accelerating its rhythm; again, the propeller struck the calm waters with its forceful wings, troubling them with eddies, whirlpools and foam; and majestically, the *Dauphiné* proudly spread the white trail of her wake over the tamed sea.

IV. The Invisible Monstraces

It was estimated that, if there was no bad weather or mechanical breakdown, a day and a half would be sufficient to regain the route from which they had been separated by a week adrift.

The steamer had resumed its progress at about five o'clock in the evening, and when dinner was served at seven, there was such enthusiasm and animation among the company assembled in the large first-class dining-room that one might have thought that Sandy Hook was already in view.

The dread, fears, terrors and despair were all forgotten, and although two places—those of the former commandant and the first lieutenant—remained empty, no one paid any heed to the fact.

At Robert Toby's table, which was the steward's, words were exchanged of this sort:

"In sum," Toby declared, "it's quite agreeable to me to spend another ten days aboard. These crossings are my only vacations!"

"Agreeable!" objected the steward. "In the conditions is which we still found ourselves yesterday! You're not hard to please."

"To be sure!" someone added.

"Evidently," Toby said, "less serious events would have sufficed for me. What you're saying to me is true. I'm beginning to find, in fact, that after having been obliged to suffer what we've endured, nine and even ten days' delay is very little..."

"To compensate for your emotion?" the steward completed.

"Bah!" said Toby, casually. "With regard to emotions, I've experienced worse, I can assure you."

"Oh, certainly," supported Hallet, a comrade of Toby's. "What's two or three deep waves[10] by comparison with a tornado, a simple tornado, or a typhoon? If you'd traveled the coast of Formosa like me, in the China Seas..."

Hallet was interrupted. They were familiar with his story of a ship struck by a cyclone, unable to escape it, subjected for five hours to furious driving and left thereafter demasted, the deck bare, constrained to throw a part of the cargo into the sea, and taking in water everywhere regardless, incapable of steering, already piling food into the launches when a savior appeared, an English steamer of the P. & O., which collected everyone and even succeeded in towing the badly damaged streamer all the way to Shanghai.

"Deep waves?" Toby objected. "First of all, there aren't any—those, tidal waves? Not on your life!"

"Sapristi!" retorted Hallet. "They're frequent enough, though."

"You've seen many of that size before, then?"

"What do you think they were?"

The steward intervened. "Generally, in fact, deep waves are more benign for ships of our size."

---

[10] The French phrase "*lames de fond*," which I have translated as "deep waves," although "seabed waves" might be more literal, has no exact equivalent in English; the reference is to an alleged phenomenon more widespread than tsunamis, and as the subsequent discussion implies, there was some controversy as to whether there really was anything substantial behind the term. It is nowadays used commonly in metaphorical terms, to refer to a groundswell of support or a force of nature.

"And then," Toby added, "there hadn't been any tempest beforehand capable of raising such waves."

"Well, what were they then?" Hallet demanded, who did not like being contradicted. "Come on, Bob, tell us what they were!"

"How do I know? A tidal wave…a submarine eruption…"

"A volcanic eruption! In these parts!" Hallet exclaimed. "If we were sailing in the Pacific, I wouldn't say no."[11]

---

[11] Author's note: "Vincent Tricard shared Hallet's opinion on this point, judging impossible the production of such phenomena in that part of the Atlantic, and attributed to Toby's story, as well as the strange details accompanying it, to hallucinations induced by exhaustion and starvation. I must confess that I had also adopted that way of seeing myself. because it seemed to me to be an effect confirmed by what we know about manifestations of that kind, when the following item, lending singular support to the opposite version, was published by the newspapers:

"AT SEA OFF NEWFOUNDLAND, New York 1 March. The steamship *Teutonic* arrived in New York yesterday after having encountered, at sea off the Newfoundland banks, a terrible deep wave, so violent, given that the sea and the wind were calm, that the officers attributed it to a submarine volcanic eruption. The ship suddenly found itself in the presence of a gigantic wave, which fell upon the deck like a cataract, penetrating between decks through the hatches. It seemed for a moment that the sea had opened up to swallow the vessel and a sharp panic seized the passengers. One of them, who was on deck, was thrown into a bulwark and suffered a broken jaw. Another had a broken leg that it was necessary to amputate. A number of sailors were badly bruised. Iron ramps and tubs were twisted and broken. (*The newspapers*, 2 March 1901.)

And a debate was engaged regarding the interpretation that it was appropriate to put on the abrupt appearance of the three masses of water that had been perceived running from the horizon to precipitate upon the *Dauphiné*. The subject was not exhausted when the gentlemen, in accordance with an old habit, went up on deck, where, perceiving that neither the lounge nor the smoking-room existed any longer, they compensated for their absence with cheerful memories.

For want of manille, they decided on a hygienic stroll.

One by one, cigars were lit.

The evening was delightful—exceptionally so, for soon, certain observations were imposed.

The atmosphere became warm, almost hot, charged with singular effluvia, like those that are hardly ever perceived except when one approaches coasts or the presence of islands is signaled. To the habitual on-board odors—hot gusts charged with the reek of oil and steam coming from the engines, the slightly sulfurous emana-

---

"Now I recognize that this description concurs very well with what Robert Toby said concerning the adventure of the *Dauphiné*, especially when one takes account of the different tonnage of the two vessels. The impartiality of which I have made a duty in commencing this story thus constrained me to publish this testimony. G.D."

The White Star liner *S.S. Teutonic*, with a tonnage of approximately ten thousand, did indeed encounter a massive wave on 24 February 1901, which was reported when she reached New York; two lookouts were dislodged from the crow's nest, but not killed; it was 9 a.m. on a Sunday morning, and there were no passengers on deck. Contemporary suggestions did attribute the probable cause to a tsunami provoked by submarine volcano, but that was pure speculation.

tions of the smoke whose back plume was curving back in cascades beneath a starry sky, emanations more directly respired now that the shelter of the awnings had disappeared—new scents were added, charged with iodine and bromine, scents of beaches at low tide, of algae evaporating their harsh perfume, and others, the putrid breath of decomposing wrack, the heavy vapors of marine mud, and yet others, impossible to classify, which corrected by a light and voluptuous charm the brutality of the former.

Illuminated by a nascent moon, the sea, increasingly calm, extended like a sheet of solidified metal, in which a strange gray tint replaced the profound blue that colors the Ocean on clear nights. At the rear of the ship, the propeller was churning up dark spirals striped with silver, sometimes traversed by brief phosphorescences, and a soft patch of oil prolonged the wake, instead of the habitual scatter of bright turquoises.

The members of the little group composed of the steward, Hallet and Toby, which had been joined by the doctor, were striding at a brisk pace over the area comprised between the companion-way leading down from the spardeck to the deck and the cord behind which the helmsman, the commander and officers of the watch were posted.

They were alone, and in the good humor that accompanies easy digestion, they were enjoying the pleasure of sensing once again beneath their feet the regular march of the engine, the trepidations by which the course of the steamer was affirmed. They were congratulating one another on the limpidity of the firmament, the torpor of the waters, the mildness of the atmosphere...

Nevertheless, separately, each of them was privately astonished for a brief moment, either pausing to re-light his cigar or ceasing momentarily to take part in the conversation, by that very limpidity and torpor. Most of all, they were sniffing the passing breeze at intervals, without communicating their surprise at the odors it was bringing.

Finally, one of them made up his mind. It was the doctor, I believe.

"I beg your pardon for cutting in," he said, interrupting Hallet, who was telling some story about a woman, "but for a quarter of an hour now..."

The others stopped dead, and the steward replied for them all: "I'll wager that I can guess what you're about to say. It smells like land, doesn't it?"

"Yes, that's right."

"One would think so, indeed," confirmed Hallet and Toby.

Hallet went on, in a surly tone the failed to dissimulate a vague fear: "Damn it! What's going to fall upon us now? To begin with, it's stupid to headed northwards like this, where we've already been caught. We ought to have made a detour."

"Oho!" exclaimed Toby, shaking his head, smiling and rubbing his hands together delightedly. "I believe that my vacation is going to be extended."

"You're cheerful!" said the steward. "Do you know that we only have just enough coal to get back? Further hitches? We'd be in trouble..."

"Bah!" said Toby. "There's enough wood here to make progress without coal."

No one made any reply.

The doctor sniffed that suspicious air, as if to discern the provenance and the quality of the various aromatic essences that it transported. Twisting his graying beard, the steward inspected the horizon, which, brightly illuminated did not offer any dangerous silhouette creating a bump in the circular line.

Hallet muttered in a low voice, stringing together oaths, and then said: "One can't expect this. Look at the sea; one would think it were made of lead...and you can smell it, can't you? You can smell it! Are those perfumes natural? No—it's absolutely necessary to ask the lieutenant whether he's sure of his course. It wouldn't be anything extraordinary if, having a jury-rigged rudder and a compass that might be out of order, we were wandering somewhat at hazard."

"But there aren't any coasts in these parts, or reefs," said the doctor. "There's no risk of encounters of that sort, and even a fairly extensive deviation wouldn't expose us to any danger. In any case, it wouldn't explain anything."

"I don't care!" said Hallet. "I want some clarification. I'm still going to talk to the lieutenant."

Naturally, the lieutenant, with the disdainful assurance of youth, replied with a smile that, under the regime of certain winds, it wasn't impossible that scents of the kind that had struck the gentlemen's sense of smell—which he had been perceiving himself for an hour or so—might be carried a long way from shores. He took pleasure in the abundance of citations with which a reliable and well-informed memory furnished him. Then he obligingly sketched out a learned lecture on the configuration of that part of the Atlantic, described the gentle slope leading from the shores of Europe to the median trench that separates the two continents, which attains a depth of ten thousand meters in places. Finally, he affirmed, after having consulted the chart, and rapidly manipulated his compass and protractor, that they had at least nine hundred feet of water beneath the keel, and showed them the day's route.

"You have no fear, then," Toby said to him, "that if the waves the other week were caused by the eruption of a submarine volcano, there might be further upheavals?"

This time, Hallet did not think of contradicting his comrade.

The physician approved, frankly: "That hypothesis seems to me to be judicious, and a geological modification of that magnitude would considerably diminish the value of your chart's indications, lieutenant."

"Pardon me, Doctor," the latter replied, "but permit me to remark that no evidence, except for a special condition of the atmosphere—a known condition, recorded by numerous observations, as I've already explained to you—no serious basis, no semblance of proof, supports that manner of seeing. Although, in the Pacific, and even in the Mediterranean, striking examples of that undeniable activity of the terrestrial crust have been quite frequently observed, in the median region of the North Atlantic, where we're navigating, our distance from the coasts, the absence of volcanoes on those coasts, and the depth of the Ocean exclude the slightest possibility of adopting such a theory. Thus, far from according that opinion a credit that nothing justifies, we ought to relegate it to the rank of an interpretation, ingenious but unconfirmed, belonging more to the domain of criticism than that of practical application.

"Since we've engaged on that terrain, it would be permissible for me, in my turn to attribute the meteorological phenomenon of which the *Dauphiné* was the victim to an entirely different cause, which, for my part, I'm inclined to believe better founded. I could invoke, for example—not without some plausibility, you will readily grant me—the fall, and then the explosion in the bosom of the liquid mass, of a bolide of considerable weight and dimensions. Falling into the sea some distance away from us, such that it was impossible for us to perceive any trace of its passage, it would then have occasioned that unexpected perturbation. That is a plausible explanation, which ulterior information might perhaps confirm. However, one could easily find others. Thus the work of..."

The lecture continued on further bases.

What do you expect? He was certainly a worthy fellow, and very knowledgeable. He had invented an apparatus that registered automatically, on beautiful sheets of graph paper, the diagram of the progress of the ship in twenty-four hours and gave warning by means of a mechanism linked to a electric bell in the commandant's cabin, of errors by the helmsman, when the axis of the ship was displaced beyond the limits of the direction given.

Very worthy and very knowledgeable, although he had a marvelous possession of the mathematical and physical sciences, he was ignorant of everything to do with human beings. He was unaware of the marvelous power of instincts, the forces slowly acquired and then conserved and transmitted from generation to generation to ensure the permanence of races whose safeguard they constituted. He was scornful of the most ancient of them all, the primordial instinct of conservation, to which, however, all of our actions are connected, and he did not suspect, in consequence, that the fear of an unknown danger is sometimes a salutary thing.

However, he ought to have recalled that he disposed of the lives of others, that the best leaders are those who surround themselves with the most precautions, use scouts, enlighten themselves in every fashion, and think that theories, instructed by slow reasoning and past gropings, only remain uncertain and transitory, whereas instinct, better alerted by its age-old education, often sees more rapidly, more accurately and further.

To the observations of the doctor, the steward—mature men—the frightened Hallet and the anxious Toby, the lieutenant offered his tranquil laughter, his erudition, his references, and the reassuring little numbers that strewed his chart.

He arrived, therefore, where he wanted to arrive...

Scarcely had the anxious group left the young man when an old crew-master who had listened, impassive and mute, to the entire dissertation and the words exchanged, approached the officer, beret in hand

"Excuse me, Lieutenant," he said, "but truly…look out there…if that's not land..."

"What! You too, Trédurec?"

"One could at least place a man on watch at the prow..."

"You're mad! Fog, and you're getting scared! Some mist..."

The crew-master simply replied: "I don't believe so, Lieutenant. I know full well that we ought to be…in open sea...wide open sea…but... At any rate…you're in command here; I can only shut up."

And he returned to the helmsman, staring long and hard at the horizon, where his experienced eyes recognized peril in a milky band that was beginning to emerge.

Half an hour later, everyone could see it. One might have thought it a mass of clouds, heaped up confusedly at the limit of the sky.

Hallet, pointing at it, shouted to the steward: "We're not going to argue any longer now with the donkey on watch. I beg you, run to inform the lieutenant who's fulfilling the functions of commandant."

The steward, without relaying the insulting element of Toby's comrade's words with regard to the officer of the watch, set off immediately, sensing the imminence of danger.

In the dining room, which had served as a lounge since the accident, he found the Commandant standing beside the piano. A young American woman was playing *Blue and Gray* with zest,[12] accompanied in low voices by a choir of her compatriots, and the lieutenant was obligingly turning the pages of the album in which the celebrated march was juxtaposed with ballads and "minstrel songs." Not far away, at a table, aged gentlemen were playing whist; at another, ladies were writing letters; elsewhere, couples were flirting. Those people seemed to have completely lost the notion of what had happened a week earlier; and when the steward had penetrated into the long, brightly-lit room, he experienced before that spectacle, a sudden indecision. He hesitated to trouble that quietude, those games, that laughter, for a few gusts of strange odors, a distant mist—perhaps a trick of the moonlight on the sea—and Hallet's gro-

---

[12] "The Blue and the Gray," subtitled "A Mother's Gift to Her Country," a sentimental ballad composed by Paul Dresser, was published and recorded in 1900 and rapidly became a hit on both sides of the Atlantic as gramophones became a popular form of home entertainment. Although the reference is to the colors of the Civil War, the song was written during the Spanish-American War, in which the hypothetical singer loses her third son.

tesque terror. The officer of the watch, de Lacour, a distinguished fellow, serious and knowledgeable, had been so affirmative, and here, this joy, this calm, seemed so reassuring...

Nevertheless, thinking that the Commandant would be able to come back down after a momentary absence, he waited until the last chord was played. Applauding the voluntary choir and the player himself, he approached he lieutenant and excused himself:

"I beg your pardon, Miss Slow..."

"Affair of service?" asked the pianist.

"Yes, Mademoiselle...oh, it's very little..."

The "Commandant," annoyed but rendered anxious by the sentiment of his responsibility, followed the steward without their leaving stimulating the slightest comment or alarm.

On the stairway, cheered up by the sound of conversations and laughter, sometimes traversed by the echoes of a foreign song coming from the emigrants' hold, the two men talked.

It was brief. As soon as he was informed, the Commandant said "Damn!" I don't understand Lacour. Double damn! As if our experience a week ago was anticipated by the charts! How do we know what's happened since? Obviously, we're a long way from the place...but damn it, a bolide! It's idiotic, believe me—idiotic!"

In two bounds he climbed up to the spardeck, sniffed the special odor, inspected the waves with a rapid glance, leapt over the rope that served as the boundary of the bridge and then, without interrogating his comrade, snatched the binoculars from the hands of the crewmaster—and as soon as he had seen the suspect clouds barring the horizon he commanded an immediate halt in order to take a sounding.

The lieutenant hazarded, in a low voice: "Come on, old man, it's ridiculous! You're going to immobilize us for an hour, wasting coal, for this joke: land in the middle of the Ocean? You think that fog over there is a coast? So what? We're more than ten miles away from it."

The Commandant adopted a dry tone to reply. "Monsieur de Lacour, as soon as you became aware that the state of the sea and the atmosphere presented something unusual, and justified, at least in part, the anxieties of certain passengers…"

"But I explained to those messieurs…"

"Don't interrupt me, please…it was your duty to notify the Commandant immediately!"

Stiffened by his authority as leader, of which the overly tragic and recent promotion had not yet permitted the usage of its power, he exaggerated the coldness of his speech, not afraid to wound to the quick the disdainful and susceptible soul of his comrade—who was possessed, for several seconds, by an intense desire to respond to that sudden and impertinent criticism, reprimanding with neither measure not pity what he, de Lacour considered to be a peccadillo, with the brutality of a definitive gesture: he saw himself striking the man who had insulted him in front of his men…

But those very men remained grave, busy with their work, and the vision of woolen jerseys and berets immediately rendered the officer to the sentiment of discipline. He constrained himself to obedience, certain in any case of his revenge as the preparations were made for the observation.

The apparatus, sealed in the deck, had fortunately resisted the impacts of the sea that had swept away everything else. It was rapidly stripped of its envelope of coarse fabric. The crew-master disposed his men, and as soon as the vessel was immobile, the steel thread unwound with a whistle that augured well.

It did not descend very far, for it had scarcely exhausted twenty fathoms than it commenced to slow down, resumed its course, and then stopped.

The Commandant interrogated Trédurec: "How much, exactly?"

"Twenty-eight and a half fathoms, Commandant."

"To starboard, now..."

A few passengers appeared on the deck. They had thought at first that it was a mechanical breakdown that had necessitated the halt. The maneuver that was taking place astonished them. Some claimed that it was perfectly ridiculous to stop to take a sounding in mid-Atlantic, and that furthermore, had it been necessary, the engine that *Dauphiné* possessed permitted that research to be carried out on the move—in which they were mistaken. Others, entirely reassured as soon as they knew that it was not an accident, interested themselves placidly in the details of the operation.

It produced almost identical results on both sides: 45 meters 17 to port and 40 to starboard...a bed of sand. At the announcement of these results the Commandant went pale, and then sent the men away.

"How much does the chart indicate?" he asked de Lacour, lowering his voice.

"Between eight and nine hundred feet...and I'm sure of the course."

"Such a difference...it's frightening."

"See for yourself..."

Forgetting the recent altercation, their former camaraderie resurgent before the abrupt sensation of common danger, the Commandant listened to de Lacour, who stacked up verifications, accumulated evidence, shifted the charts, and feverishly inspected the instruments. Neither of the two men could resolve himself to believe that those familiar servants, those precious guides, had deceived them, suddenly precipitating them, and all the lives confided to their guard, toward the abyss.

V. The Moving Land

Still seeking to convince themselves of a possible error, they were both checking their hasty calculations when clamors burst forth, rending the calm night with appeals and cries. Then they saw the deck around hem invaded by gesticulating groups, uttering the howls of beasts fearful of the impassive sea. Men were sketching gestures of menace, dispensing themselves in a mime of combat, revealing the energy of supreme despair in the contractions of their horrified faces. Others were contemplating the inevitable with pupils dilated by suffering, a mask of passive anxiety, a trembling a terrified resignation, like an animal at bay. Oaths and imprecations responded to prayers. Women were weeping, punctuating their sobs with shrill plaints.

Trédurec arrived.

"What is it?" said the officers, their hearts instinctively sinking under the same flux of anguish unchained by the clamors

"It's that if the *Dauphiné* has stopped, Commandant, it's scarcely perceptible…because we're drifting even so, unless..."

He clocked his fingers and shook his head, involuntarily. "Unless…it's that satanic coast coming closer? Damn…one no longer knows. The depth diminishing…one can see the island…and the passengers are frightened..."

"The island! The coast!"

This time, the young men were not tempted to raise objections. Even de Lacour understood that nothing could prevail against the brutality of a fact, and the fact was manifest, careless of all implausibility, enormous and tangible, increasing by the second...

At present, the ship seemed to be descending very slowly toward the entrance of a large bay, the promontories of which rose up soundlessly to either side, less than five miles away. Masking the horizon, the mass of suspect clouds designed, higher in the sky, a chain of mountains with sharp ridges, brightly lit.

The Commandant did not linger to gaze at the strange and moving spectacle that was terrorizing the howling crowd.

"The route we've been following is free. All we can do is head south...and quickly!"

But as he was about to have the order to start the engines transmitted, and give the decisive thrust of the tiller himself, the steward stopped him, and in a voice whose tone wavered in spite of the man's efforts to remain calm, he said: "Too late!"

Everyone fell silent: the passengers declared a truce in their lamentations, for the same stupor, simultaneously ecstatic and fearful, strangled their throats...

From everywhere, rocks emerged, some of them jagged reefs, bristling with points like mouths opening over sharpened teeth, others flat, broad and thickset, like gleaming carapaces, sly reefs almost at surface level; and, invading the circular horizon, preceded by a recrudescence of exhalations in which bases, bromine, chlorine and iodine, reinforcing with their acridity the heavy, miry vapors of mud...announced by a life of quiverings and stirrings that animated the sea, whose broad black waves were undulating more urgently, breaking against the impediment, gliding along the flanks of the ship, with no sound other than a lugubrious splashing...surging from the Ocean with capes, gulfs, strands, specified by the cold glare of the electric light poured forth by the moon…clad in a prodigious mantle of reflections, embroidered by scintillations, heightened by phosphorescences, traversed by flashes, reverberated by the waves that united their gleams with the image of the sky strewn with stars…streaming beneath a monstrous and unheard of adornment, of diadems of algae dominating the crests of plateaux, necklaces of marine tress scattered over the slopes, garlands of wrack festooning the plains, sculpted jewels of tortuous flights that damascened them, alloying the gold of gleaming backs and the silver of scaly armor, mounting there the bronze of brandished pincers and the gems of peduncular eyes…a sly and magnificent enemy…raised to the supernatural by the prestige of its perfumes, the sparkle of its lights, the quivering of its agonies…from everywhere, toward the silent vessel, the moving Land advanced...

"Too late," repeated the steward, quietly.

"Yes…too late," repeated the Commandant, his brows furrowed, his mouth twisted in anguish.

A detonation responded to him.

He turned round abruptly, and saw Lieutenant de Lacour lying on the table with the papers in disorder; he had just fallen backwards, amid the maps and the instruments.

A trickle of blood was running from his right temple, and his hand had not let go of the revolver of which he had made use.

At the sound of the firearm, echoes awoke.

The immense hemicycle, the steps of which continued their ascension, took possession of the dull sound in order to end it back from wall to wall, and prolong its resonance until it was confused with a multiple symphony that seemed born of that appeal and ensure that it did not fall silent.

Powerful voices, bellowings and sonorous clamors rumbled.

The deluge of a thousand cascades threaded along the slopes, with laughter, gurglings and hiccups that fused between the seaweeds; and they also began to hear the high voice of waves, unfurling ponderously against the recent soft beaches that the Ocean abandoned. Expelled by that slow rise, of which it was the conclusion, and which was now transforming its slight into a seething of unquiet waters, by turns plaintive and roaring, sometimes the sea wept, sometimes it howled, in precipitating itself against the breakers and rushing toward the narrow channels still ending in open water.

It flowed impetuously there, like torrents after a storm. It dragged away, in its leaps, blocks of granite that collided with tumultuous impacts.

It ferried the furious music of herds of frightened beasts, the tails of which struck the foam of the whirlpools, fins clicking desperately in the eddies, powerful tentacles stinging the current with their lashes, and the savage harmony of forests of strange plants, uprooted, noisy, that it bore away in its demented course...

The *Dauphiné* had to moor with two anchors in order not to be thrown against the rocks.

Scarcely had the last chain been paid out than an aged officer, cutting through the crowd, irrupted on to the "bridge" and planted himself before the "Commandant." It was the chief engineer.

"I won't answer for anything any longer," he said. "My officers can't keep their men at the boilers and the engines any longer. And then, I don't know myself what it's necessary to do..."

The Commandant could hardly hear him in the midst of a frightful din.

"We've stopped!" he went on. "Until when? And what's that racket? Where are we? Even if we let the fires die down, if we stay here for a few more hours, we'll find ourselves short of coal..."

"I can't tell you anything, Santony," the Commandant replied. "It's necessary to wait for daylight."

"Wait!"

"You can see for yourself that we can't go any further forward before having reconnoitered those breakers, sending a launch to sound..."

"How did this happen?"

"Oh, very rapidly, I sure you."

"Very rapidly! But damn it, we must have run into this impasse—who was on watch, not to have seen the hornet's nest into which we were digging?"

"It was Lacour."

"And..."

"Here he is," said the Commandant, taking a step back.

"Oh my God!"

"He killed himself when the last issue closed."

"Ah!" Santony looked at the cadaver, and then went on: "I spent all yesterday afternoon with him to get his recorder back in working order. He wanted it to be ready, since the rudder had been installed...and this morning, again, he was so glad, dipping his stylet in the ink. I remember now...before going up to take his watch, he asked me to make sure that all of our new contacts were functioning, if the clockwork apparatus was sufficiently regulated, if all was well...if all as well! The poor boy...he was worth better than this end!"

"What do you expect, Santony?" said the Commandant. "The chart showed nine hundred feet...nine hundred feet at this very spot. Could one foresee the accident a week ago, in which we nearly sank, and that it would be followed by this rise in the sea-bed by which we find ourselves imprisoned? How could he have known?"

"It doesn't matter—it would have been better to take a sounding two hours earlier and to live! Then again...he's taken the shortest route. Perhaps it's the best one. Anyway! Do you think it's necessary now to put the fires out? And what shall I tell the men?"

"The truth."

"The truth?" The chief engineer looked around slowly, better able now to discern the enormous amphitheater, and then the bottleneck, barred by reefs.

"The truth," he said, "is that we're trapped like rats, and on all sides. Damn! The truth...is that it'll need dynamite and months of work to establish a pass."

"Get away—in daylight, we'll find one."

"Do you really believe that we'll get out of here one day?"

"Whatever happens, our duty is not to doubt it. Last week we came through an ordeal rude enough for us to hope to triumph this time too."

The old engineer turned his head, and pointed at the coast. "Look at those peaks that are growing, those craters from which the water is spurting, boiling! Listen to the thousand thunders howling. It's really finished, this time! One slightly stronger convulsion, a little less water yet, and the ship will come apart on her own..."

"It's necessary not to say that, Santony! You mustn't even think it!" said the Commandant, violently. Then constraining himself to be calm, he continued: "Go

back to the engines. Only leave the indispensable personnel with the engines. Let everyone rest. Tomorrow..."

"Tomorrow! When that short stop has sufficed for
the route to be cut off! Tomorrow!

"Certainly!" The officer's tone expressed absolute
confidence. "I have a firm conviction that we're only
blockaded temporarily. Our arrival has probably coincided with the ebb-tide, and our halt has prevented us
from departing with the tide, which was already lowering and is still lowering, as we can hear it going out, but
which will return in a few hours. At any rate, we're
afloat. Why despair?"

This time, Santony made no reply; he would have
had said too much. He went back to his engines.

The throb of the steam in the boilers, as soon as it
was heard, moved him like the plaint of a domestic animal in pain.

Nevertheless, he went down by the narrow steel
ladders, shiny and greasy, shirting the monsters at re-
pose.

As he was surrounded again by the hot atmosphere,
which presented the customary visions to his eyes: lanterns whose crystal eyes were awake, cylinders with
shiny tops maintained by large screws to the robust
flanks circled with copper, to the metal limbs lubricated
by the greasers, awaiting oil, an infinite sadness filled
his soul and weighed upon his breast.

Perhaps the death of Lieutenant de Lacour had impressed the old engineer thus? Perhaps there also entered
into that sentiment a painful apprehension, caused by the
necessity of telling the men he could see confusedly beneath him, looking out for his return with anxious faces,
about the futility of their recent efforts? Perhaps also
mingled within it was the reflection of obscure presenti-

ments, the shadow of an intuition stronger than the Commandant's reasonings? But above all loomed the regret, the bitter regret that his cares as a good leader, the quality of his auxiliaries and the power of the engines, reconquered, had only obtained for their ironic salary leading the *Dauphiné* meekly to the precise point where fatalities awaited her! A delay of one night, and the trap would have been avoided!

On the bridge, after the successive departure of the steward and the physician, summoned in haste, Hallet and Toby had remained isolated in the middle of the growing crowd, participating in the successive emotions of the passengers, without reacting individually, without being able to transmit any impression to one another. The operations of the sounding had preceded by too brief an interval the appearance of the moving Land to permit them to grasp it; then the tragic detonation, unleashing a formidable tempest of noises, doubtless because it coincided with a fine quake, which finished emptying, with a great din, the immense bowl that had emerged from the Ocean, had drawn them definitively into the same vertiginous anguish that was maddening all the souls aboard.

Nevertheless, when Hallet saw Santony quit the bridge, his head bowed, his shoulders slumped and his back curbed, he grasped Toby by the arm. "Now, old man, that's it!" he declared, in a hoarse voice. "You heard the chief engineer: one more quake, and we're done, completely done!"

"You're ridiculous, with your fears," replied Robert Toby.

"I'm an idiot, am I? And a little while ago, I was just as idiotic when I affirmed that it was absurd to head northwards. In sum, did they think of that? We wouldn't have ended up here…and we'd be out of it!"

"Oh, from here...we'd need at least two hundred miles."

"So? That doesn't alter the fact that I was right. Damn, damn, damn!"

"What! As long as we have water under the keel, there's no reason to despair. Then again, if we're retained for a few days in the limits of this island…and even more than a few days…a long time, I'll admit…would it necessary to be desolate for so little? On the contrary; it will be admirable: the weather's good, summer's coming..."

"No! You're talking seriously?"

"For sure."

"I don't understand you."

"Think about it. What's the worst we're risking? Being stranded. In that case, this land will be very rapidly discovered and out absence signaled. They'll send a steamer to search for us, and it will be all over."

"Unless it happens as the other feared…that before the night is out, the ship will be gutted. Well, what if we have to go through the terrors of the other day again? And who knows what might yet happen. I'd rather..."

"You'd rather what?"

"Throw myself in the water right away."

"Get away, you fool! Would you care to shut up! It's finished, this. I assure you that it's finished. We can no longer hear anything extraordinary. We're no longer budging. See whether those people are afraid!"

Around them, in fact, as all immediate danger seemed to have been avoided, that the ship was once again reduced to a reassuring immobility, and was favored by the calm of a splendid night, the terror of the first moment had given way to a nervous release that was translated in bursts of gaiety, sounding here and there very loudly, tearing through the quiet voice of the elements. Pleasantry was rubbing shoulders with admiration, with occasional returns of anguish, quickly dissimulated, which immediately destroyed the confidence of neighbors.

Some declared that, in sum, since there were neither numerous deaths to deplore nor any damage to register, by comparison with the frightful surprise suffered last week, this one would simply be tedious—they had certainly been making thirteen knots—disturbing the plans newly established; and yet, did it not offer compensations? That was what others suggested.

Thus, in a joyful group, the same one that the steward, an hour before, had seen listening to *Blue and Gray* being played with so much zest, which had taken up a position near Hallet and Robert Toby, someone said: "Admit that the adventure isn't banal, and that we ought to congratulate ourselves for having been the nearest witnesses, in the best seats. If we had only bumped into some unknown rock or an unknown island..."

"In that case, Jack, my friend," a young woman interjected, "we'd probably never have known, for your unknown rock would have rapidly left us in no state to divine its presence in these parts."

"Forgive me, Miss Slow: I was only thinking that if it had already emerged, if it had been visible at a distance, it would have been less marvelous to salute a new land than to witness its birth."

"In truth," Miss Slow said, "it is grandiose! Even now, look at those currents interlacing like black and white serpents, those strange cliffs throwing off a thousand sparks like precious gems, those mountains raising their summits toward the sky! It's marvelous, unprecedented, magical! Oh, what miserably petty things those adjectives are before such a spectacle!"

There was an explosion of bravos and laughter. Then another young woman, taking Miss Slow by the waist, said: "And remember, Jane, what Mr. Diver said. Remember that we're certainly the first, and doubtless the only, people to whom it has ever been given to contemplate such an event! It seems that we're recommencing a very old story, a story of the initial times of the world; it's the end of the Deluge, the waters retreating, Listen to them fleeing with rage!"

"Yes, yes, we can hear!" cried the chorus of young men.

"Now they're abandoning the summits, and soon the Ark will run aground—the Ark that contains the hopes of a new world."

"Oh, Marjorie," objected Miss Slow, "what a horrible prediction!"

"Please," implored the masculine fraction of the group, "can't we modify the denouement, and take the Ark within sight of Brooklyn Bridge?"

"What?" she replied, scandalized. "What are you asking? Do you really not know that Mount Ararat was the last port of call of that navigation? Modify the denouement…take the Ark further on…but my dear boys, that's impossible!"

At that moment, Hallet murmured to Toby: "These people are definitely mad. I don't know what's holding me back from fleeing them forever..."

"No stupidities, I beg you."

"In any case, I don't want to stay here, listening to that. I'm going!"

"Excellent idea, old man! Let's go play a hand of manille in the steward's café!"

"Joke as much as you please. Me, I'm off!"

"Where to, you triple idiot?"

"Oh, no matter where. I've had enough!"

"Come on, come on...calm down," said Toby, linking arms with his comrade, holding him tightly. He sensed that Hallet was close to executing his project of suicide, out of weariness, to avoid having to tremble again before new opportunities for fear. He led him away like a child, saying to him in his most natural tone: "You're right. Let's not stay here. It's time to go to bed. After all, it's getting late, and well—cascades, rocks, foam, it's always the same thing!"

They stopped at the foot of the main stairway. A sailor had just finished pinning up a manuscript notice on the dining room door. Toby read it aloud.

"Notice. The Commandant of the Dauphiné, desirous of avoiding any anxiety on the part of the passengers, believes it his duty to bring to their attention that he will proceed, tomorrow morning at dawn, to take soundings, with a view to locating the channel by which, according to all appearances, the ship entered at high tide the bay where it is presently at anchor, and the presence of which, at a point indicated as virgin on the charts, it is permissible to attribute to the recent seismic disturbances.

"Once the reconnaissance of the indicated passage has been obtained, the ship will be set moving with the precautions that the circumstances require. The passengers are therefore invited not to be alarmed, either by a possible prolongation of the present situation, or the maneuvers to which the aforementioned operations will give rise, or, finally, to pauses susceptible of occurring in the course of resuming navigation. The Commandant. Signed: Laffite.

"Well," Toby interrogated, when he had finished, "are you reassured now, you poltroon?"

Hallet looked at him obliquely, groaning: "Damn it! All the same, I'd give a lot to have these tricks finished..."

They reached their cabins, while groups were forming around the placard, whose terms drew sufficiently favorable comments.

On the lower decks and in the emigrants' hold, the same communication had been pinned up.

Thus, in spite of the decreasing hubbub that continued to envelop the ship with confused noises, the population of the *Dauphiné* slept tranquilly for the remainder of the night, save for the men on duty and the chief engineer, who was keeping vigil over the body of Lieutenant de Lacour, in company with the steward.

The reflections of those two remained pessimistic.

VI. The Lieutenant's Launch

Someone came into Robert Toby's cabin, approached the narrow bunk, considered the sleeper momentarily, and then sighed deeply and shook him, murmuring: "Bob! Hey, Bob, wake up! Wake up!"

"Eh?" said Toby, his eyelids fluttering.

"It's me, Hallet."

"All right, all right."

"Come on, wake up."

Toby started. "What's the matter now? And what the devil has brought you out of your bed so early?"

"I can't sleep any longer, since it's getting light."

"And you felt the need to prevent others from sleeping."

"Forgive me, Bob; I'm scared."

"Of what?"

"I'm afraid. In the middle of a typhoon, I wasn't as frightened as this. I've never been as scared as this."

"But for what reason?"

"I don't know. I can no longer hear anything except the footsteps of the sailors up above. After yesterday's racket, the silence frightens me. It's not natural. And the boat hasn't budged, you know. So what the Commandant had pinned up, the tide…and the rest…it's false! The prow ought to have shifted…"

"It's to tell me this nonsense that you…"

"Toby, I beg you, get up! Come up on deck with me. I want to know. Here, I'm too frightened; I'm stifling. It seems to me that at any moment, we're going to sink, to be swallowed up. Never, I repeat, have I felt such emotions, and yet I'm not on my first voyage, am

I? Well, I'm scared; I'm atrociously scared. There! And if you had a heart, you'd understand me, you wouldn't be arguing..."

Toby sat up. Was Hallet going mad? Or were his fears justified?

His comrade's terror, which had seemed to him, at first, to be absurd, now infiltrated him. After all, the position of the *Dauphiné* remained sufficiently abnormal for a catastrophe still to be feared.

Hallet's fearful manner, his ruddy complexion replaced by a network of violet threads on an ashen background, eyes in which the pupils were immeasurably dilated, reducing the iris to a thin gray circle, his lamentable attitude, slovenly jacket, the shirt sift and crumpled, before which hung a badly-knotted cravat, the trousers descending like corkscrews toward the slippers, all the grotesque details of that silhouette became pitiful.

Toby stood up at ran to the porthole.

Through the narrow round opening a dawn of adorable colors was perceptible, strewing with pale violets and pinks a landscape that Bob could hardly make out through the fog.

Above the waves, long rails of gauze unfurled, lightly tinted with red by the dying aurora. They fled toward indecisive mountains, establishing a magical décor from which an exquisite calm emanated, an embalmed freshness. The tumult of the day before, appeased, concluded its extinction in a murmurous splashing, little different from that produced by the ship's matinal toilette.

Behind Toby, Hallet, collapsed on the divan, retreated: "All this will end badly. For sure it will all end badly."

Reassured, Bob turned round. "Come on," he said, laughing, "stop moaning! Daylight's coming. Boats will probably be put to sea, and we'll soon know how we stand."

"I tell you it will end badly," Hallet repeated, obstinately.

"Oh, no! It's impossible that they won't find any point of exit. In spite of the mist, one can make out torrents flowing into the bay; it's necessary that they get out of it! In any case, one can already recognize the lines formed by the currents..."

"Listen!" Hallet interjected. "What are they doing?"

A crew-master's whistle modulated a summons. Bare feet could be heard running on the deck. A steam-powered windlass rumbled, coughed, spat through its open release-valves, fell silent, and then resumed rumbling; and the heavy friction of an unrolling cable shook the ceiling of the cabin.

"Exactly what I said—they're lowering their boats," Toby observed, after a pause.

"But...what if they're going to abandon us, to escape without us? Come quickly, Bob! Come, I beg you!"

"What baroque ideas you have this morning!"

"Toby, have pity on me! My fear's taking hold again..."

Bob shrugged his shoulders, and said, in a resigned tone: "At least let me get dressed. You know that they won't be ready as quickly as that."

"No! I'm going up...I need to know."

"That's all right. Go find out! That way, I can get dressed in peace..." And Bob took off his pajamas.

Hallet's absence did not last long.

Toby had scarcely finished shaving when his comrade returned, his face even more livid than when he departed, ad threw himself on the narrow divan, muttering in a dull voice: "The rabble! The brigands! It's as I foresaw! Oh, was I an idiot this time too, Bob? Well? Guess what work they were doing when I arrived!"

"I don't know."

"One boat was afloat. As for the other, they were renewing the fresh water in its barrels, loading it with fresh food supplies, tins of preserves, bottles—everything that the lockers of a launch can hold!

"I saw the first boat set off in the direction of the open sea, with the Commandant himself! Fortunately for us, as they were sending out the lieutenant's boat, they stopped. I interrogated a sailor. At first, he didn't want to say anything. Finally, I learned that it had a hole, and that it had to be checked out at close range, the other day's waves not having spared it...but those wretched imbeciles were in such a hurry to get away from us that they hadn't suspected it until the last moment. They're repairing it now. Oh, they're not embarrassed; they're no longer in a hurry; the provisions are aboard. And before fleeing, if any passenger asks, they'll say: 'You know very well—the Commandant's notice, the soundings! We're going to proceed with the soundings.' Then they'll decamp, like the first.

"But we're warned, the two of us, my old Bob. It's therefore a matter of not letting ourselves be played. They'll be busy for an hour at least; that's enough time to reflect, and make a decision. What do you think?"

Toby, who was washing himself at his bowl, raised his streaming head and reached for a hand-towel. "Bah!" he replied. "I think...I think, simply, that you're exaggerating."

Hallet leapt up, overexcited. "May I be damned if I've said a single word of a lie!"

"I'm not saying that you're lying. You're exaggerating, that's all."

"That's right," Hallet declared, his face darkening. "There's none so deaf as those who refuse to hear. I repeat to you that I've seen with my own eyes those casks and food supplies, that I've seen them stowed in the boat, as I'm seeing you."

"So?"

"Naturally, I'm stupid to tell you that, since you're obstinate in not believing me. But that's all right! I'll see what I have to do."

"Triple idiot!" uttered Toby. "Your poltroonery has reached the point of not being able to understand the simplest things. Is it necessary, then, always to transform the smallest incidents into subjects of terror?"

"Yes! Yesterday's odors… simple incidents of the route; our imprisonment here…an even lesser incident; these provisionings…"

"What? You don't imagine, perhaps, that they're going to launch people into an unknown sea, in unexplored regions, without furnishing them with the regulation supplies, and even a small supplement."

"Since they're presumably remaining within sight of the *Dauphiné*?"

"Ah! And what if they can't maintain communication with the steamer, if a wind rises that's too strong, if there are currents too violent, which draw them away, if, in that case, their absence is prolonged—a day, two days, a week—is it you who's going to take them something to eat?"

Hallet made no reply.

However, Toby sensed that he was not entirely convinced. He looked at him for a moment, torn between a scornful disgust for the wretched marionette, unhinged by fear, and a sentiment of commiseration for that distress. It was the latter impression that prevailed. He said to him, in a calmer tone:

"Go back to your cabin. Finish dressing. We have time, since you've said that the repairs will need at least an hour's work. Come to get me afterwards; we'll have breakfast. One has clearer ideas when one's ballasted a little. Then we'll take stock."

"You consent to try, then…?" said Hallet, joyfully.

"Yes. We'll see about that in a little while."

In reality, Hallet's terror was beginning not only to make Toby anxious but also to shake his own confidence, the equilibrium of a cheerful individual inured to the unexpectedness of travel, accustomed to adventures, and inclined, moreover, by a natural mental disposition never to accord malignity even to the worst events.

Nevertheless, in the present circumstance, while rejecting the ideas defended by his comrade, retaining the intimate conviction of a man who thinks, unlike a Hallet, that everything will sort itself out in the end, there remained from that conversation a shadow of suspicion, an imprecise mistrust, against which he could not entirely defend himself.

It often happens thus, that, in spite of our belief in the poverty, the lack of foundation and the implausibility of certain arguments, we find something within us that continues to combat in our contradictor's stead, and which sometimes triumphs in spite of our disdain, in spite of our reason, simply because we tire and they persist, incessantly returning to the attack, indestructible, and registered mechanically.

Robert Toby was balanced between this thought: *If our situation continues much longer, that animal Hallet will end up going completely crazy*, and this reasoning:

Why, in fact, are they taking two boats out of the remaining three? And why do they need so many provisions, if it's really only a matter of exploring a bay whose dimensions are scarcely ten miles? Might Hallet, this time, not be mistaken?

Toby became anxious.

VII. La Pascalieri

For the first time in the crossing, when he was at table with his comrade in the long dining room, where they found themselves the only guests at that hour, Bob ate distractedly and without pleasure.

Having nibbled his last slice of toast, he drank a swig from the cup of chocolate that he had in front of him and wiped his mouth with his napkin ill-humoredly.

Hallet buttered further slices, looking at him from time to time with an anxious expression, not daring to chat.

Toby took a cigarette out of a case that he had extracted mechanically from his pocket.

At that moment the head waiter arrived, affably offering him a lighted match.

"By the way, Monsieur Toby," he said in a confidential tone to Bob, whom he had known for a long time, "I ought to warn you: my tobacco supply has run out."

"That's annoying!" Toby declared.

"Let's be clear," said the head waiter. "It's run out…officially, but you can imagine that for you I'll still have a box of cigars, and as many cigarettes as you need. Only I'm no longer giving them to anyone else, except the officers. We habitually only bring enough for a journey back and forth, don't we?—and, well, as you know, it's nearly twenty days since you set out!"

"And we're not yet on the eve of our arrival," said Toby.

"As to that, no, But…are you going up to see the boats set forth? The Commandant's has already started the soundings."

"Yes," Hallet interjected, in a bitter tone. "As they were about to lower the lieutenant's, they noticed that the other day's damage hadn't been repaired. It's unfortunate, all the same, to think that in case of need, we wouldn't have been able to make use of it immediately."

The waiter sketched an ironic gesture of negation. "Pardon me," he said, "but that's not entirely correct. You've doubtless been poorly informed."

"What!" exclaimed Hallet and Robert Toby, at the same time

The waiter drew nearer to the two men and whispered: "To tell you the truth, someone has spun you a line, Messieurs."

"Eh? Impossible!" exclaimed Toby.

"Word of honor! Anyway, you can take it for granted that they didn't wait until this morning to check the state of the only three boats we have left."

"What is that one waiting for, then?" asked Bob.

"A passenger."

"A passenger?" the two men repeated, Hallet at the peak of anguish, Toby, whose doubts were reappearing.

"Well, yes. She isn't ready. It's a little early, isn't it, for a lady?"

"But who is she?" asked Toby.

"Oh, I don't believe you know her." The waiter inspected the dining room before continuing. No one had come in. A junior waiter was sitting somnolently on a bench, far enough away from the talkers. He went on, therefore, leaning over the table that separated Hallet and Toby.

"It's a beautiful girl, an Italian singer and dancer—in sum, a café-concert star, La Pascalieri, who has an engagement for a tour of the America music halls. She's always remained in her apartment—she had two cabins on the deck—and she nearly stayed there forever, for, as you know, at the time of the accident everything was flattened. By an extraordinary stroke of luck, she was down on the second at the time; she'd gone down there to see her chambermaid, who was ill. You remember that everything was battened down for the cyclone, and in consequence, she was forced to stay there until the evening. Then, she was installed in a luxury cabin on the first, but she continued not to mingle with the other passengers, having herself served in her cabin and only going up on the spardeck at night.

"Now, since there's no more bridge, you'll understand that the rope wasn't a serious barrier, and that the proximity of a pretty woman, with the aid of solitude..."

"It was easy to engage in conversation during the hours of the watch," said Toby.

"Precisely. Today, the beauty has probably thought it very amusing to go on an excursion with her lover; I've prepared a cold lunch for them, champagne..."

"Oh!" said Toby, then. "Mightn't there be an opportunity to profit from the opportunity to take a little trip?"

"Oh, with you, Messieurs, who are free and independent, they wouldn't be embarrassed. You'll risk nothing by trying. She seems very amiable, and as for him, he's a very polite fellow."

"In fact...him?" Toby queried.

"He's the only lieutenant remaining, since poor Monsieur de Lacour..."

"Ah, it's Laffite?"

85

"No, Monsieur Laffite is fulfilling the functions of Commandant. It's the third lieutenant, Monsieur Rogés."

"Rogés! I know that name. He isn't the Philippe Rogés who served on the Antilles line's *Auvergne*, by any chance?"

"Yes—two years ago."

"That's it. Then all will be well."

"It's all right, then? He wouldn't have done it in the time of the former Commandant."

"Bah! There's no one up at this hour...they'll come back at night...and then, what harm are they doing?"

"Oh, it isn't me who'll criticize them," Hallet declared.

"All the same, thank you for having told us," said Toby, shaking the head waiter's hand "Opportunities for distraction are so rare."

"*Bon voyage*, then!" the latter relied, smiling. "And don't spare the provisions—I've been generous!"

"Aha!" remarked Hallet. "Thanks."

"When he was alone with Toby, he said: "You see! The lieutenant is planning to run away with his mistress. What luck, eh, that we were suspicious! Provided, at least, that he'll agree to take us with him?"

"Rogés? He'd like nothing better."

"You think so?"

"I'm sure of it."

When they left the dining room, the two friends headed for an open panel, beneath which a fully-prepared boat was waiting. They did not go any further.

It was one of the large lifeboats that could hold thirty people. At present it was carrying four crewmen and a cabin boy. Next to them were a few gaffs, oars and ropes. At the freshly-rigged mast, a new sail was flapping in the rising breeze. At the fore, a jib was ready to be hoisted. Neat the tiller, a blue carpet, fringed with red and decorated in the corners with the company's arms, was covering the rear storage-locker.

There was nothing in the boat that was not absolutely normal, and yet Hallet's unquiet imagination found in each of those details a further confirmation of his fears. For him—and Toby was no longer so far removed from his ideas—the excursion was a pretext, La Pascalieri's amour one proof more, demonstrating clearly the reality of a escape.

What finished convincing him was the attitude of the officer himself.

He arrived alone, and seemed surprised and annoyed at first on seeing the two men. Then, as soon as Robert Toby had reminded him of their former acquaintance and exposed his request, he hastened to say in a cheerful tone: "Certainly, Messieurs. Embark, I beg you."

Then the boat drew away slowly, without the passenger announced by the head waiter having appeared.

Toby and Hallet exchanged victorious winks. So even that story, fundamentally, only dissimulated a means of obtaining fresh food, masking with his feigned gallantry the shame of a flight! The officer had recoiled from an argument, and had immediately admitted the two men, in order that nothing would stop him at that decisive moment. As for the absence of La Pascalieri…he cared very little about that!

VIII. The Western Pass

At present, daylight had arrived, with oblique rays gliding over the waters, helming the waves with gold and surrounding with light the somber forms of the anchored steamer.

A thin thread of yellow smoke was escaping from the funnels and, driven by the wind, massing in a transparent cloud in the depths of the bay.

The coasts were more clearly perceptible, high cliffs with unexpected colorations of coral and amber, and gray beaches, occupying the horizon on three sides.

To the south-east, behind the ship, the other boat could be distinguished, a little white patch like a seagull, maneuvering in the sunlight between the uneven lines of reefs gilded by the light.

Then, even further away, there was a confused bar cut by foam, dark liquids, low and obscure silhouettes that dentellated with minuscule notches the milky blue of the sea.

The boat flew, with the wind behind, in a gentle murmur of skimmed water, heading for the mysterious land, toward the unknown of its beaches and promontories.

After having moored the sheet to the mizzen and put down their unnecessary oars, the sailors, at an imperceptible sign from the lieutenant, went forward, disappearing on the other side of the sail, whose inflated canvas formed a kind of screen.

The cabin boy remained. He took a silver-annealed and gem-encrusted cigarette case out of the pocket of his reefer jacket and, having opened it, offered it to Hallet and Toby.

"Please do, Messieurs," he said, in a slightly hoarse foreign accent, with a light laugh.

Only then did Hallet and Robert Toby notice the marvelous rings that ornamented the pale fingers of the little hand, the admirable eyes animating the oval of the slightly cold mischievous face, its fresh complexion stimulated by the morning breeze, the very red mouth...

It was La Pascalieri.

With her supple, slender, ambiguous body, her short dark curly hair, bouffant beneath her straw hat with a broad ribbon, she had played the role of a boy marvelously.

The lieutenant was amused by the alarmed expressions of the two men, whose disturbance he attributed to the unexpectedness of the revelation. Then, looking at his mistress, now sitting next to him in a pose of familiar abandonment in which her feminine grace reappeared, which could not be dissimulated this time by the disguise and the cigarette, he said, tenderly: "Don't you think she's adorable like this?"

Hallet grimaced, murmuring: "Madame is certainly charming."

"More than charming," Toby added, with vivacity. "Madame has just proved to us that she's as witty as she is pretty."

"I'm confused, Messieurs," said La Pascalieri. "So many compliments at once! But...Philippe?"

"That's true," said the lieutenant. "Pardon me, I should have introduced you sooner...

"Monsieur Robert Toby, an amiable passenger from the *Auvergne*, whom I'm delighted to meet again aboard the *Dauphiné*. Monsieur...?"

"Eugène Hallet," completed Toby, who added: "As for Madame Lina Pascalieri, we have had the pleasure of applauding her very often already, without suspecting that hazard would one day furnish us with an opportunity to tell her how much her talent has delighted us."

"The hazard is fortunate for me," La Pascalieri replied, "but in all frankness, I must declare that I have favored it somewhat. The idea of this excursion was mine. It was really from me, in fact, that the idea came of going for a little trip, when we don't know where we are or what might yet happen. In any case, it was very wicked of me to have demanded it of poor Philippe."

The lieutenant thought he ought to explain. "I haven't dared to leave the bridge at night. On the deck, in the frightful tumult that only died down later, we—Lina and I—were watching the foam fly away in the moonlight; we were listening to the surf roar, with the constant idea that it was the end of everything, that the frightful cataclysm wasn't going to end without engulfing us all, and that we wouldn't see daylight again...

"What a night! A night of vertigo, hallucination and nightmare! Those mountains, presently so bare, so wild, so desolate, with their brush of marine plants, shining then with a thousand phosphorescences, filled with cries, exhaling excessive perfumes and sometimes seeming to be summoning us with their innumerable blinking eyes, their roaring voices and the seduction of their breath!"

"Truly," said La Pascalieri, in her turn, "you can't imagine what temptation pushed us toward them. So I begged Philippe to promise me that if we were still alive today, he'd take me out there. Now, that seems crazy to me. They're no longer like those of the night: they're dirty, somber, silent…but how they attracted us! How urgently we wanted to climb them!"

"Yes," said Rogés. "At dawn, when the pilot relieved me, I hastened to ask my comrade Laffite for permission to equip a launch and take it to land, even though the port of call wasn't foreseen and isn't regulation!"

"Oh, I'm glad all the same," said La Pascalieri. "I'll wager that we're going to see marvels. Isn't it true that the land must hide marvels?"

"Undoubtedly," Toby advanced, content with the denial that the adventure inflicted on Hallet's prognostications.

"Personally," the lieutenant objected, "I fear that we'll encounter more seaweed and mud than treasure."

"No, my love, don't say that! Remember that these mountains have emerged from the bottom of the sea! Is that possible, eh? We've seen it, however. So, perhaps we'll be walking on a carpet of pears and coral; we'll discover rocks of gold and ruby, caverns of sapphire, and we'll play at throwing diamonds into the sea to make them skip...clear, round diamonds, slightly flattened! That will be beautiful, it will be amusing."

And La Pascalieri clapped her hands, like a child. Then suddenly sad, she said: "How slowly we're advancing. One might think that the mountains were retreating and didn't want us to approach them. They really are retreating—look!"

"It appears so, Madame," said Toby, "but if you'd care to look at the *Dauphiné*, you'll take account of the fact that we're making progress, and traveling quite rapidly."

Diminished in size by distance, the steamer, devoid of masts and rigging, offered the aspect of a small pontoon anchored at the entrance of a harbor of which, at that distance, the entrance seemed free. Nevertheless, the boat, which was now in the middle of the bay, was still a mile or two from the far side of the vast amphitheater, where it was gliding over calm water, now inundated with light.

Gradually, details became more precise.

It was possible to distinguish the coast toward which the launch was heading more clearly: a rather broad strip, designing a kind of perron, where green patches maculated a leprous, ashen clay with flecks of silver, separating from the sparkling mirror of the waters a bright bronze cliff incrusted with pink marble. It rose up toward the sky like a giant wave suddenly prettified in its surge.

Outcrops projected from the ensemble, rocks carpeted with strange mosses, decorated with red festoons, hollowed out by indentations of a paler hue. Buttresses raised their stout pillars toward the crests, covered with light brown arborescences. Elsewhere, a confused tangle of marine plants combined colorations ranging from crimson to coral, and here and there among the heaps of those chaotic masses, the snow of cascades inserted the smooth whiteness of their falls.

Then a cutting appeared, quite clearly, toward the west; another also raised its black line to the east. The wall that appeared to close the bay possessed breaches, then!

A singular emotion gripped all the souls aboard the little boat, which continued its insouciant course, illuminated by the sunlight of a radiant morning. Standing at the prow, a sailor pointed out the two gaps to his comrades. One of them was heard to say: "Well, the others are sounding to find a pass, but we've found one before them!"

The lieutenant had taken a pair of binoculars from the locker. "He's right," he said, after a summary examination of the terrain. "What we can see is doubtless only an island, and we could certainly have doubled it, at least to port, for in that direction, not only does the channel open broadly, but the corridor seems to broaden out increasingly."

Disdainful of these realities, La Pascalieri hazarded, in the voice of a sulky child: "When are we going to land?"

"We left the *Dauphiné* early enough for us to be able to dispose of a few hours without urgency," Rogés replied, "all the more so as the cliffs we can see mustn't be an easy climb, with their sheer walls, and the masses of seaweed we can divine. They don't offer a goal for a very tempting excursion. In addition, the beach that extends at their foot is probably muddy, to judge by its appearance, and in consequence, not very propitious for a disembarkation."

"I want to land anyway," she said, furrowing her heavy eyebrows.

"I'm entirely disposed, my dear Lina, to give you satisfaction. Nevertheless…Christopher Columbus asked his crew for three days…just grant me an hour, and perhaps we'll then discover…."

"The route to the Occidental Indies!" put in Robert Toby.

"…A less inhospitable location," the lieutenant completed.

"Oh, if only you were both telling the truth!" sighed Hallet.

He had pronounced that sentence in such an anxious and lamentable tone that La Pascalieri burst out laughing, and, becoming insouciant once again, a mocking cabin boy, she said: "Oh, Monsieur, don't demand so much of them! A pretty corner of sand to have lunch in the shade, that would be sufficient. And then, visiting a few grottoes populated by unknown and savage monsters, the ascent of a mountain from which one can see the entire archipelago, and on which we'll trip over gold nuggets, which we'll disdain to pick up…there'll be too many, won't there? And then again, gold is so heavy!"

Meanwhile, the lieutenant had set a course for the opening clearly designed in the west. The jib was hoisted and the speed of the boat accelerated, because the wind was brisk.

Soon they were skirting banks of hardened mud, chaotic heaps furrowed with profound crevices, naked in places, in other places presenting mounds covered in thick green tresses, mingled with a rough crust of debris.

They traveled for some distance alongside rocks whose granite disappeared beneath an inextricable tangle of wrack and mosses, still damp.

Enormous stalactites formed by an interlacement of uprooted vegetables swayed here and there, with reflections of emerald and topaz and diamond scintillations, gigantic tufts suspended from the edges of anfractuosities, draped themselves by curtains of bloody lianas.

Elsewhere, one might have thought there was the face of a bronze statue, studded with monstrous veins, animated with frissons by the muted life of the torrents that streamed over the mask.

Some slopes, in the vicinity of the crest, displayed singular meadows of long grass, flattened on the ground, as if by the trampling of herds or the passage of squalls.

Suddenly, a cry resounded, uttered by La Pascalieri.

"There! There!" she stammered thereafter, pointing to a spot close to the boat.

They all looked, and what they saw, through the troubled water, obscured by the mud in which the sunlight was dispersed in minuscule golden spangled, was a double colonnade of broken and blackened stumps, raining their fluted fragments in quincunxes. At a thrust of the tiller from the lieutenant, the boat slowed and changed direction, and veered almost into the middle of the buried avenue.

It seemed as if a recent inundation had submerged those ruins, and everyone sought to glimpse the distant crumbled palaces to which they ought to lead.

Hallet was the first to think that he had found one. "To the right, behind the second mound: a staircase!"

"Oh, Philippe, let's stop" La Pascalieri asked Rogés.

The officer had the sails lowered. By means of the oars, they circled the banks. A few moments later, the boat stopped before a broad causeway, strewn with fallen columns, the disposition of which in long and narrow steps depicted quite well the stairway identified by Hallet.

"It's fantastic," said Toby. "But where are we, then?"

"Let's disembark, let's disembark quickly!" the young woman implored.

"Futile," Rogés replied. "The steps only lead to a platform of sand..."

"Perhaps we'll discover statues there, jewels and vases," she said.

"It would be necessary for that for this really to be the site of an ancient city...and in spite of their sculptural appearance, I very much fear that these columns and steps aren't the vestiges of a vanished city."

"What could have sculpted those black stones like that, though?" asked Hallet.

Rogés leaned over, and examined a stump near the launch, half-covered in mud.

"I knew that it reminded me of something…it's simply basalt; they're needles of basalt. We were rather easily taken in, all the same, eh?"

"Oh, right!" said Toby. "The Giant's Causeway…I know that. You must be right, but…it's a pity!"

Meanwhile, La Pascalieri put her upper body over the edge, leaning further forward; her hand finally reached the ground, and briskly picked up a small object. She showed it to Rogés.

"And is this basalt too?" the singer demanded, handing him a small polished stone, a dull turquoise green, in which the accidents of structure produced excrescences, depressions curved, ridges and planes. The ensemble sketched a vague resemblance to a feminine figure, seated and draped—a resemblance nevertheless uncertain, as Rogés remarked.

"It requires a considerable prejudice," he said, laughing, "to discern anything human in this mineral fragment. And the hole of sorts that perforates what one might regard as the head, what's the meaning of that?"

"Exactly," said La Pascalieri. "It's an amulet, and the hole must serve to suspend it from a bracelet or a necklace…"

"What a vivid imagination you have, my dear! If you don't mind, we're going to resume our route nevertheless."

While La Pascalieri contemplated the deformed figurine, so strangely encountered, with a superstitious emotion, the boat drew away from the ruins, leaving the basalt palace to starboard, and reached the western pass shortly thereafter.

It moved into the channel.

The water there became deep, and abandoned the opaque, dark, almost black tint that it conserved in the bay, to take on a milky transparency, streaked with indigo. An unexpected current slowed the progress of the vessel.

The various indications observed by the lieutenant indicated, according to him, the existence of a communication, via that strait, between the bay in which the *Dauphiné* was anchored and the Ocean.

He pointed out hopefully the little waves that the breeze was raising, and which splashed against the prow, covering the front of the boat with spray.

Then the waves became calm again; the wind ceased to blow, blocked by the screen of the land. The sailors were obliged to row.

In its turn, the sun disappeared behind the cliff.

Then La Pascalieri, who had begun to launch the first couplets of a song against the grim walls separated by the liberating breach, abruptly fell silent, and huddled against Rogés' side, in the fashion of a beautiful fearful animal taking refuge beside its master.

After her, no one any longer dared to awaken the lofty echoes of those solitudes, which only reverberated with the sound of the oars bumping the copper of the rowlocks and striking the virgin waves...

How long did the journey through that passage last?

None of the individuals borne by the launch were ever capable of estimating it.

The men had continued rowing automatically, without the sweat on their faces having alerted them either to their fatigue or their anguish.

All of them agreed on one point: as soon as the face of rock had extended its wing of shadow and the last syllables vocalized by La Pascalieri had died away, they had felt a kind of dolorous stupor, a numbness against which they remained impotent to struggle. Each of them was frightened by the faces of his companions, which had become white and spectral, expressing a horror that all of them were experiencing within themselves. Pale lips were twisted in a rictus; shudders contracted the visages hideously.

Then there was nothing: an abyss, a void that left no memory.

How did the boat continue its route regardless? How did it not break up on the reefs bordering the channel? How did those it carried find themselves sailing between flat banks, burning with the ardor of the tropical midday sun?

"Toby didn't explain it," Vincent Tricard told me. "He merely recalled that the first action that fooled their reawakening was laughter: an atrocious, inextinguishable laughter that shook them with convulsions."

The men let go of two oars; they drifted away without them hazarding a movement to pick them up, without the lieutenant uttering a word of reprimand…and the hilarity didn't stop: a demented hilarity, without a cause or an object, which quickly became painful, finishing in spasms, hiccups and asphyxiated gasps.

The second fact that Toby subsequently recovered in his memory was the transformation of the sounds and the perfumes.

On the other side of the pass, the splash of water against the sides of the boat, the moaning of the ropes and the canvas in the wind, and the rhythmic noise of the oars had been the only punctuation of the silence of a morning traversed by marine exhalations, embalmed by humid scents.

Here, the returned breeze brought a murmur of foliage, like that of an immense forest whose branches were colliding and whose foliage was swarming with perpetual shivers. And Toby also recognized the odor, the perfume that, the previous evening, had tempered with its trance, unknown, voluptuous charm, the bitter reek of the tide and the mud.

No woods however, no clumps of trees, displayed their branches, no verdure patched the golden robe of sands beyond which now, in the west, the four lines of foam of the crests of four perpetually renewed waves, succeeded the assault of the strands, underlining with their parallel undulations the last margin of the Ocean, occupying the horizon.

To the east, a bare terrain rose up, pleated by large creases, all the way to mauve hills. Perpendicular to the wall of rocks, a breach in which the launch had just come through.

Toward the north, the lagoon in which the boat was located curved abruptly, losing itself behind one of the creases in the ground. In that direction, the dome of a high mountain plastered a screen of violet silk over the satin blue of the sky.

Gradually, within the boat, attitudes became normal. The lieutenant had the sails hoisted again. The mariners wiped their brows, gazed with astonishment at the oars, two of which were missing; some dipped their hands in the water. They dared not talk to one another.

"Toby," Vincent Tricard reported, "claimed that he had a passionate desire to interrogate his companions, to discover whether they had also felt the strange impressions. But he assured me that, at the idea of carrying out that natural and simple action, he had experienced the same repulsion as if he had been on the brink of committing some frightful sacrilege, capable of attracting an immediate and formidable punishment upon the entire group."

Why was it necessary not to talk about it?

He did not know.

It was absurd, certainly, but more powerful than his reason or his will. He noticed that La Pascalieri stretched herself with the slow and lovely gestures of a she-cat, that her eyelids fluttered when she opened her mouth to say something, an exclamation that she did not pronounce, doubtless obedient to the instinctive dread that dictated a unanimous silence to those various souls.

Except that she took Rogés' head in her hands and kissed him on the mouth for a long time, in a fit of furious immodesty—which, moreover, according to Toby, did not shock any of the spectators of the scene, who would, on the contrary, have been revolted by the slightest allusion to the disturbances that the traversal of the western pass had marked.

Hallet was the first to make an observation, to which no one objected.

"There's the sea," he said, pointing at the immense expanse, sparkling under a sapphire canopy. "There's the open sea."

It was a relief to hear a human voice.

"It's hot," said La Pascalieri, in her turn, in a weary tone. "One can scarcely feel the breeze, and yet the sails are inflated."

"We won't stop here, then," the lieutenant replied. "Further on, perhaps we'll find a little more freshness.

"Then we'll have lunch, I suppose?" asked Hallet. "I don't know if Madame is like me, but I'm beginning to feel quite an appetite."

"What time is it, then?" asked La Pascalieri.

"I can't tell you the exact time, Madame," Toby declared, "but like Hallet, my stomach is making demands, and seems to indicate that it's long past midday."

"An effect of the open air. We set off very early, and..." Rogés did not continue, for at that moment he had to maneuver in order to steer round a bend.

At that point, the lagoon became a channel, ceasing to skirt the broad beach and the Ocean.

Once again, the lieutenant inspected the desolate surroundings that we were quitting. He reflected for a few seconds, and then said: "What a contrast there is between these plains of sand and hardened mud, and the luxuriant marine vegetation of the cliffs that enclose the bay where we were sailing this morning! The difference between the two landscapes must surely be explicable.

"The rise in the sea-bed must have been produced slowly back there, slowly enough for all the marine flora whose abundance was so striking to prosper on the rocks for years, perhaps centuries, whereas here, this crust of scarcely-dried mud was surely beneath the waves less than a week ago, doubtless at the depth shown on the charts, and I suppose that the convulsion that raised it up one day with the same surge as the amphitheater in which the *Dauphiné* is confined caused those frightful waves from which we nearly perished last week. And that was what Lacour couldn't have foreseen!"

"However," Toby objected, "didn't we see that bay emerge from the sea yesterday evening?"

"Yes, we witnessed the ultimate, most clement quake."

"You think, then," Toby persisted, "that at the moment, we're looking at a terrain that was covered by nine hundred feet of water?"

"I believe so."

"It's lugubrious," declared Hallet, "with its chalky banks, wrinkled like an elephant's skin. Fortunately, I hope that the excursion will end here, for the route we've been following doesn't seem to lead anywhere."

"Wait," said the lieutenant. "A bend is sufficient to mask the route, it isn't significant that it's been interrupted."

"But we can't see any foliage, or seaweed, or streams," said La Pascalieri. "Where is the noise we can hear coming from?"

"That's true," Hallet confirmed. "One might think we were on the edge of a wood. Now, according to what you've said, it's improbable that we're approaching any trees, unless we suppose the existence of forests composed of unknown species susceptible of growing nine hundred feet under water."

"As we don't know what that rather high undulation in the ground curving ahead of us, or the mountain gorges, conceal, it's difficult to be informed at present," Rogés replied. "If we were on a river, though, I'd swear that there are rapids over there, near the peak." Then, pointing at the flecks of foam that were beginning to surround the boat, floating in the direction of its progress, he added: "Look, we're being carried by the flow. I'm sure that the sands that were interposed a little while ago between us and the Ocean are submerged now."

"We might be able to reach the open sea again, then?" Toby queried.

"We might. As for the *Dauphiné*, it's scarcely probable that her draw will permit her to use such a passage, even if she's partly unladen. Pay attention! Here's the bend that Monsieur Hallet considered to be an insurmountable barrier... Well, you can see, Monsieur, that we're not obliged to return to the *Dauphiné*. Of course, there's only just enough room to steer...oh, just!"

The hills, in fact, formed a new bend at that point, at the elbow of which the launch almost touched a bank that narrowed the channel.

IX. The Perfume of Lust

After a quarter of an hour of progress without further incident, they emerged into a creek strewn with islets and surrounded by high buttresses, such that one might have thought it a shaft hollowed out in the mountain itself and half-filled in by landslides.

A uniform livery of ash-gray, striped with white lines of scintillating crystals that had been deposited there by the evaporation of the salt water, dressed the escarpments that were staged by circular ledges, continuing to rise up in the direction of the peak in broad steps, in the fashion of a stairway constructed for giants.

Those quasi-geometric forms did not fail to surprise the passengers in the launch by their regularity; but they resolved immediately to utilize that disposition of the terrain, which, by virtue of the superimposed terraces, lent itself easily to climbing, initially choosing one of them to use as a dining room, in order to profit from the shade, the coolness and the perfumes accumulated in that place, and saving the other successive platforms until later, with the objective of obtaining some information about the new terrain that hazard had permitted them to discover.

That program, suggested by the lieutenant, had been accepted with enthusiasm, and was immediately put into execution.

La Pascalieri wanted to disembark first.

When the young woman had jumped, with a light bound, at the sound of the little varnished shoes striking that virgin soil—in spite of the childishness of the gesture, the made-up face of the singer and her disguise, mingling operetta with epic, in spite of the intimate skepticism of Rogés, Hallet and Toby, and in spite of the leaden indifference of the sailors—all the men in the launch felt a strong and sudden emotion: the joy of capturing a prey, the pleasure of taking definitive possession, and the pride of a marvelous conquest.

The intoxication of ancestors resuscitated in them an ardor long abolished, seething in their veins. With foolish exclamations and laughter that multiplied the echoes and drowned out the murmur of invisible springs, they launched themselves in turn, joyful and puerile, taking pleasure in marking their footprints forcefully in a soft and elastic clay, and breathing in the air of the banks deeply.

It was more abundantly saturated with singular effluvia, vaguely discerned since the day before, and they felt an impression difficult to definite, which had something of vertigo, of oppression, and brought with it the instinctive shrinking of being before the unknown, even when attractive.

The seduction of that strange philter prevailed, however, easing their fears. The drank deeply from the immense cup in which he familiar reek of tidal water and wet sand became apparent beneath the light weave of the irritating perfume. The latter was reminiscent of ambergris, musk and carnations, perhaps participating in those various odors, possessing the delicate essence of one, the animal potency and the embalmed flame of the others. And yet, those comparisons remained insufficient and pale. Other and new, its mysterious scent was intoxicating, in the fashion of ether. Thus, the woman and the men felt sharp sensations there that immediately marked them with a common stamp, engraving profoundly in their souls an imprint different from those that the various experiences of life had so far deposited there.

They perceived the shock of it, and, as their companions on the *Dauphiné* were to do subsequently, attempted to rebel as soon as they had noticed that in that furrow, scarcely opened in their most secret selves, vivacious plants were already germinating, threatening to corrupt and stifle the efflorescence rooted in their former selves.

But one cannot avoid an atmosphere; one can only deliver oneself from the emprise of an environment by flight, and here, for the moment, escape was impossible. In any case the prison was offered ornamented with delights, and in spite of the unconscious, involuntary and organic recoil of the initial moment, and then the attempted reaction of the first reflection, it was above all the vision of charm that was dominant within them.

"That, Monsieur," Vincent Tricard said to me, "doubtless seems incomprehensible to anyone who has never witnessed the considerable transformations that a simple change of latitude can inflict on the personality of an individual."

I suppose it is worth recalling that precisely because of Bob's divagations—to use the term employed by Tricard—he conserved of those revelations, in fact, the image of a nightmare lived, or rather dreamed, by his comrade Robert Toby during the fever and delirium to which the castaway had fallen prey in the dinghy that the *Hulda* encountered. The circumstances of time and place that produced those confidences were, if you remember, a night of tempest and fog aboard the *Normannia*, which had contributed to fortify that judgment in Tricard, by attaching to the memory of the story, for him, a persistent association of memories, also associated with the fantastic and the unreal—if one excepts what you will remark of the obscure, and what has been, for my part, impossible even to imagine, inspiring, for the rest, facts of current observation that that he had easily been able to observe in himself and on others, in the course of his voyages.

"In Africa, a European, as you know, easily become a ferocious brute, no longer finding the spectacle of blood and dolor repugnant, and the same white man who, in Paris or London, would strike a coach-driver brutalizing his horse, will maltreat some unfortunate negro out there with the worst tranquility, if not pleasure. In Asia, he will go in a different direction; it is sensuality that increases, although the influence of those regions is always double."

"Obliterating at the same time, if I understand you correctly, the median measure of pity and modesty that a normal civilized being possesses."

"Exactly."

"And morality—what becomes of that is all of this?"

"Morality, Monsieur, I would gladly compare to a garment. Evidently, we don't wear the African loincloth, the Hindu turban or the Japanese robe; in those countries, however, we adopt the pith helmet and the white suit."

"Assimilating virtue to an overcoat that one puts on or takes off according to the temperature is a rather bizarre comparison!"

"I don't want to cite you examples here, on this steamer, even though…but on the India line, everyone will tell you that after Colombo the captains had a great deal of trouble preventing their boats becoming true..."

"Tricard, please!"

"Wives of petty functionaries, employees, and no matter what, who would have remained honest all their lives in Europe are pinched—like the others. As for the men...hang on, I've talked to you about Choupot, an old comrade of mine, whom I encountered aboard the *Normannia* at the same time as Bob...if he's now associated with a *compradore* and will never leave Canton again for as long as he lives, it's less to earn a few piasters than because he encountered a woman out there who holds him. She's dirty, ugly, with lacquered teeth, greasy hair, a chignon in the form of a boat...she smokes opium...but there you go! The sun, what! And the spices, the odors...everything!"

"The odors. It's true that they possess over us, from that point of view, a greater empire that we suppose, and since ancient times, courtesans have known that power and have used it. So it was, in fact, the perfume that had...impressed Robert Toby?"

"Well, after a few minutes, neither he nor the others paid any further heed to it. The head waiter had done things well: folding tables and chairs, linen, crystal glasses, cold meat, fruit, gateaux, champagne, liqueurs...that lunch lacked nothing—according to Bob, that is!"

"Yes, yes...leave me the illusion that it really happened like that."

"So completely that at dessert—was it the famous perfume? was it the champagne?—the diners forgot that they were on the arid and desolate flank of an odd mountain, in an unknown archipelago, quite a long way from the *Dauphiné*. Even the sailors, who had been handed a few bottles and cognac in the launch, were as drunk as Poles, and didn't take long to fall under the benches."

The applause of Rogés, Hallet and, who were fêting La Pascalieri, going though her repertoire, didn't wake them up...

On the broad and shady clay terrace overlooking the waves, the young woman sang, very provocatively, only interrupting herself to cover her lover with kisses.

She dispensed, said Bob, as much debauchery, leering and lewd gestures to underline the filthy lyrics as if all the steps of the mountain and the rocks of the creeks had been boxes garnished with spectators, and the sheet of water enclosed between the escarpments a floor black with a crowd, and she performed in front of that desert and those three men as if before a packed hall.

That crazy excitation did not preserve her from fatigue—was it fatigue, or a pretext?—but she couldn't have foreseen what would happen...

After one final couplet, one final dance, without any other orchestra than her fingers, clicking like castanets, she performed the splits in a salvo of bravos, footstamping, and pretended to stay there, exhausted, lying on the ground, while Rogés, Hallet and Toby beat a frantic ovation on the table with knives and forks. La Pascalieri's reefer jacket was open; the plastron had slid down, uncovering one of her breasts...

Then, a strange scene unfolded…

One might have supposed that the singer mimed, with an uncommon artistry, an excessive verity of attitudes, some gallant adventure: she was surprised in bed, still asleep, and there was an abrupt awakening, astonished and wild at first, pert and exquisite thereafter. The offering of a spray of flowers was accepted, an embalmed apology…no, not an apology!...a prelude to enterprising attempts, against which she defended herself, laughing, refusing her lips, turning her head, opposing ripostes, dome of them voluntarily weak, of an extraordinary realism.

Then her face became animated. Her eyes shone more…

And the three men understood only then that her perfect performance had nothing imaginary about it; for suddenly, a communication as unexpected as it was complete was established between them and La Pascalieri!

"I don't know, Monsieur," Vincent Tricard added, "whether you really understand what Bob meant by that? He affirmed that not only did he seem to be in intimate contact with that woman throughout his flesh, and that she, Hallet and Rogés were experiencing an identical impression, but also that that contact at a distance, that special and sharp touch, extended to movements, and that *he could also hear the thoughts of the singer and those of his companions*—those are his own words. Now, you might well suppose that the sound of that orchestra was not at all disagreeable, and that the bizarre communion of flesh and souls offered a few charms…!"

"A doubling of the personality? Perhaps a collective hallucination..."

"I don't know how one can define it, exactly and the precise terms that are appropriate. There was, in sum, La Pascalieri lying down, and the other three who, without quitting their place, were executing with her the worst inventions that were dictated to them by the most frightful lust. Now, the singer appeared to be receiving the caresses of all of them and rendering them to each one, augmented by her triple desire. Her respiration accelerated. Hr visage was pearled by sweat. Soon, she threw off with urgent movements the various pieces of her masculine disguise, until she was entirely naked, writhing in the poses of intercourse, embracing the void with her arms...but at every gesture every embrace, the three men shivered with the same frisson, for they felt in an irrefutable manner the supple loins of the young woman rearing up forcefully; her fluid skin was really running through their fingers; and her warm arms really were clutching them to a breathless bosom..."

Successively, Hallet fell backwards, clawing the ground with his fingernails, prey to a crisis of sobs and moans...Rogés hid his face, his arms beating and scoring against the table...Toby leapt to his feet, howled an oath, then sat down again mechanically, no longer understanding, bewildered, vaguely ashamed...while, weary, after one last spasm that stiffened her swooned body, which was dotted with minuscule red bruises, La Pascalieri lay there, motionless, lascivious still, her heavy eyelids lowered, as if to sleep.

Momentarily, only the murmur of invisible forests or springs, the sound of waves beating the walls of mud, and the heavy respiration of the sailors asleep in the launch beneath the terrace, along with Hallet's lamentations, troubled the silence of the solitudes.

Afterwards, Toby saw the singer crawl like a brown snake toward the little patches that her scattered vestments put upon the platform. The whiteness of lingerie was substituted for amber flesh.

At that moment, the lieutenant raised his head. Immediately, he fixed his eyes obstinately on a glass of Bordeaux that he held motionless between his fingers, constraining himself to observe the play of the light of the crystal facets.

After having whimpered for a long time, Hallet finally shut up.

Robert Toby claimed that nether alcohol, nor hashish, nor opium had ever procured him sensations as extraordinary as those that he possessed during those minutes.

In the fashion of the light that withdraws at dusk from a landscape whose details are immediately drowned in shadow and buried, one after another, under an increasingly thick veil, the singular faculty of perception suddenly projected into his mind, after having brought about that exceedingly precise intimacy between La Pascalieri and the three men, between himself and the others, gradually became obscure.

In isolated gleams, similar to the returns of clarity on cloudy nights, a few brief touches still persisted, scraps of strange ideas reached him. Those last brushes, those ultimate thoughts of others were:

My God, have pity on me! I have sinned... That emanated from Hallet.

Tre... Tre...per Bacho! Me, cheat? Yes, yes, my love, I swear to you... And no one would ever believe me! That from La Pascalieri.

One tumultuous phrase immediately followed it in Toby:

I'd have to kill that woman and those two men...and blow my brains out afterwards, if that filthy orgy were anything but a dream...and it's already too much to have dreamed such debauches!

A sound of breaking crystal rang out sharply. Lieutenant Rogés had decapitated the glass he was holding in his hand while putting it back on the table violently—and Robert Toby, at the slight pain in the index finger and thumb in his own right hand, knew that the young man was continuing to clutch the stem that remained in his fingers, violently.

Hazard determined that Toby lit a cigar. The smoke, it seemed, dissipated the charm very rapidly. Hallet ran to slump into a chair. La Pascalieri, dressed again, approached the table, and someone who passed by at that instant would not have perceived anything except three fellows placidly savoring their havanas, and a young cabin-boy drinking liqueurs.

In the same fashion as on the subject of the torpor and the anguish suffered at the entrance of the western pass, once again they dared not exchange reflections. No allusion could be risked.

Only La Pascalieri, sniffing her fingernails, which were tarnished by gray mud, said, with an equivocal smile: "Decidedly, I believe that the enervating perfume we've been breathing since yesterday impregnates the earth itself. And yet, there are no flowers to be seen..."

X. The Prison of Sand

The shadow extended, enveloping the peak with a large black mantle from which all that emerged was an enormous round head, brightly illuminated.

Around the table on the terrace, the bouquet of alcohol and the blue smoke of cigars had reconstituted a familiar atmosphere, and the freshness increasing with the fall of dusk contributed to a salutary relaxation, returning calm to minds and bodies.

They discussed the possibility of an ascension.

Hallet, supported by La Pascalieri, opined in favor of an immediate return to the *Dauphiné*, fearing that they would not reach the ship before nightfall.

The lieutenant wanted to take advantage of their presence at the very foot of the mountain to attempt to scale the summit and thus obtain precious information about the island—or, rather, the scatter of islets—in the midst of which hazard had placed them.

"We'd know immediately in which direction we might search for a pass, for there's no archipelago without straits—and wouldn't you be glad to take good news back to the ship?" said Philippe Rogés.

"A pass!" growled Hallet. "With regard to the pass, have you thought about one thing?"

"What?"

"What if the pass has already been discovered? What if, at this very moment, they're preparing to depart."

"They'll wait for us," said Toby.

"Ha ha! They'll wait for us? Until the retreat is cut off? Like yesterday. No! Don't believe that!"

"You're frightening me," said La Pascalieri. "And you," she said, harshly, to the lieutenant, "what do you think? Will they really have the time to remain at our disposal? And in the contrary case, would they abandon us like that?"

"I think"—and Rogés lowered his voice—"that whatever happens, you won't be able to get the men to go back to the *Dauphiné* by the route that we took this morning..."

No one made any reply, for in all of them, the lieutenant's words had evoked the flood of horrible emotions that were attached to the memory of the singular traversal of the western pass.

"That's true, and I myself..." La Pascalieri did not finish the sentence she had begun. She went on, swiftly: "What are we going to do?"

"Ha ha!" said Hallet. "That's very good... You think, Monsieur, that we ought not to think of retracing the route that we took..."

"Evidently," Toby interjected. "You know why."

"I know," Hallet went on, "that Monsieur brought us to this place, and that now it's a matter of getting out of it..."

His irritation had increased. He was speaking with the muffled voice of a man who is unsuccessfully dissimulating his anger, and seems to be chewing disagreeable phrases in order better to savor their bitterness.

"It's a matter of getting out," he insisted. "You hear me, Monsieur?"

"I can hear you perfectly," Rogés replied, very calmly. "Nevertheless, I dare to make the observation to you that I didn't ask you to accompany me. I was happy to accede to the desire expressed by Monsieur Robert Toby, whom I have known for a long time and whom I hold n high esteem. But as for you, Monsieur, what entitlement authorizes you to permit yourself to give me orders of a kind, in an ill-disguised form? Know that I alone have the right to command here!"

Hallet, forgetting that it was to his own fear that he owed having embarked on the lieutenant's launch, and seized once again by the mad terror that counsels poltroons to the worst audacities, went on in a violent tone: "Words, words, Monsieur! And you won't get anything with words. The fact is that it was simply a matter, when we climbed into your boat, of an excursion to the depths of the bay, and that, in spite of us—I take Madame as a witness to it—you engaged us in that damned pass, where we have been victim of I don't know what devilment, where we might have sunk hundred times, to the point that I now dread entering it, that evil pass that was supposed to procure us the open sea for the *Dauphiné* and has only led us in reality to this no-less-satanic mountain! That's the truth!

"Now, the responsibility for that crew—yes, that crew—on whom is it incumbent, I ask you, if not you, Monsieur? And I have the right, I imagine, to ask you, since you have taken it upon yourself to assume such a responsibility, how you intend to palliate the consequences?"

"We're in agreement, Monsieur. I accept that responsibility fully; that is why I remain a good judge of the measures to be taken."

"What are those measures?"

"Those which it pleases me to adopt...and I don't owe you any account in advance."

"That's very good! Very good!" growled Hallet. "However, I warn you, Monsieur le Lieutenant Rogés, that if we're not in sight of the *Dauphiné* in three hours, I shall blow your brain out!"

Abruptly, he pulled out a large-caliber revolver out of his jacket pocket.

"You're insane!" cried Toby, throwing himself upon him and trying to disarm him.

"Let me go, Bob, or I'll fire right away!"

"Let him go, Monsieur Toby," said Rogés. "It's never necessary to worry about these details."

La Pascalieri shrugged her shoulders and said: "Philippe, the man is right."

The lieutenant did not reply to the comment. "We're wasting time needlessly," he said. "If you want to accompany me up there, Monsieur Toby, let's go."

La Pascalieri said: "We're staying here, then?"

"Perhaps," replied the lieutenant. "That depends on the result of our expedition."

"Anyway, I don't care!" she said, filling a glass with vintage champagne. Then she began to intone a popular Neapolitan song.

Hallet took out his watch, put it on the table, placed his revolver next to it, with the butt beneath his right hand, and declared: "You have until ten past five, Lieutenant Rogés."

The officer had advanced to the extreme edge of the platform. From there he hailed the sailors, to whom he gave a few brief orders.

Two men soon appeared on the terrace, one carrying a pick-ax and a spade, the other ropes, a gaff and signaling disks.

Then Rogés began, along with Toby, to climb the second step. The mariners followed them.

The ground was dry and resistant, a kind of concrete composed of hardened mud mixed with stones;

here and there, it presented projections sufficiently solid for a foot to be placed on them without anxiety. The ascension thus proved quite easy, all the more so as fissures also cut through the chalky surface, offering multiple points of supplementary support. Their shady bands were opposed by brilliant seams of salt.

Soon, the table and its white cloth, crystal glasses and bottles, and Hallet, rigid in a pose of hallucinated attention, his eye fixed on his watch and his right hand never quitting his weapon, and La Pascalieri, a little cabin boy with a cavalier air, sprawled in a chair with a cigarette between her lips, became minuscule toys animating the arid décor. The round creek where the launch was afloat, with its two motionless mariners, was reduced to the proportions of a large bowl of somber water.

Further away, Toby and Rogés discovered a few metallic reflections disseminated between the undulations of the ashen ground: arms of the sea or channels. A corner of the Ocean appeared between two slopes. The mauve hills perceived in the morning designed the buttresses of a plateau that extended westwards.

As the sailors lagged behind, Toby said: "I'm truly confused by my comrade's attitude. In truth, I fear that the *Dauphiné*'s adventures during these last two weeks have impressed him more deeply than they should have, and I sometimes wonder whether he isn't on the point of losing his mind."

"Oh, the sun is sufficient, as you know, to provoke a certain impressionability that's hard to avoid."

"He's accustomed to tropical climates, though, and we're at a latitude..."

"Where the temperature is beginning to become treacherous."

"That's right; I'm not very reassured on his account."

"You can be tranquil. In spite of his threats, I don't think he's dangerous."

"It's necessary that I keep watch on him, all the same, for he's very overexcited."

"It's certain that for a weak brain, we're traversing strange moments. The adventure of the steamer allowing itself to be surrounded by a slow rise in the sea-bed; that tragic night yesterday, frightening and enchanted; and this morning again, the phenomenon of the western pass, and then..."

Rogés stopped, leaving his sentence suspended—but Toby knew what he wanted to say. Then, without transition, the lieutenant asked him: "Do you have a cigarette?"

"Here," said Bob. "The perfume is more expressive at this height, isn't it"

Rogés hesitated momentarily before replying. He struck a match, aspired a few puffs of smoke one after another, and finally said: "That's better... Yes, I find that singular odor is...antipathetic as well as agreeable, two things difficult to conciliate—but I'm sure that you understand me.

"There must be decomposing vegetables down there, like peat, a permanent source of volatile aids, of a formula that isn't familiar to us, ethers whose effect can be particularly pernicious. Undoubtedly it's to those vapors that we owe the sort of lethargy that overwhelmed us as soon as the launch entered into the gully."

"And that extraordinary murmur?" Toby interrogated.

"One could, in fact, believe that we were skirting the edge of a forest or the course of a stream of fresh water."

"Although we haven't perceived anything thus far that could furnish us with a solution to that mystery."

"Certainly—and although I remain fundamentally convinced of the possibility of explaining that succession of adventures in terms of natural reasons, it's evident that we seem to be adrift in fairyland. Lina would say that the archipelago is enchanted…and believe it!"

Toby smiled, without continuing the conversation.

In any case, they were penetrating the zone that the sun still illuminated, and although the star's rays were already oblique, their heat was still painful. Reflected by the bare ground and the thousand splinters of salt crystals, it rendered the ascension more and more fatiguing.

The two men were obliged to pause. They sat down on the edge of a step in the shelter of a block of hardened mud, and waited for the mariners, delayed in their progress by the weight of the tools and equipment they were carrying.

When Rogés and Toby turned their heads, with a common thought, to look at the summit of the peak, it did not seem to them that they were much closer to it.

"Damn!" said Toby. "If we want to climb all the way to the top, it won't be comfortable."

Meanwhile, the panorama that deployed its variously colored tableaux beneath them was enriched by new landscapes. Without replying to Toby's remark, the lieutenant examined them.

Suddenly, he uttered a cry of surprise. "Sapristi! Might that imbecile have guessed right, by chance?"

"What is it?" asked Toby, looking in his turn. In the chaos of plains and escarpments, sparkling channels and bays, with the green sheet of the Ocean in places, he could not find any points of reference by which he could get his bearings, nor any elements susceptible of helping him to comprehend the significance of the lieutenant's words.

"That's too much, damn it! Come on, Laffite wouldn't have done that! And yet..."

"But what is it?" Toby repeated.

He widened his eyes, fixing them successively on the mauve hills and the plateaux they supported, the strands on which the sea unfurled in waves of milky jade, the valleys cut by sinuous lines of deep blue, sometimes troubled by a glaucous reflection, the unknown gulfs, the distant cliffs...and the desolate mountains, the plains of sand or mud told him nothing...

"What it is," the lieutenant replied then, hastening his words, because they were beginning to hear the painting breath of the two sailors, "is that, firstly, we're imprisoned in the middle of an archipelago that, on these three sides at least, doesn't offer any issue. The three principal islands form a kind of lobster claw, without any other breach than the breakers before which the *Dauphiné* was moored last night, and from which we drew away this morning. You remember...the beaches uncovered at low tide. Between the two arms of the claw, formed by the reefs, is the mountain on which we are now, a host of islets and the bay where the steamer stopped yesterday evening. Secondly, I can make out that bay quite clearly, with its edges rendered darker by their vegetation, but as for the *Dauphiné*, it's completely absent, however implausible that might be! And yet I'm sure that she hasn't been able to reach the open sea..."

"Perhaps we'll be able to see her from the other side of the peak? Perhaps, too, a passage exists back there?"

"Shh!" said the officer, swiftly. "Shut up—here come the men."

In the circumstances, Lieutenant Rogés showed a calmness that the moment rendered very similar to heroism.

In the tormented panorama, striated by gullies and crevices, blistered by desolate eminences, the tangle of undulations, mounds, plains and waters, a single image imposed itself on his gaze: that of the great bright patch extended between the jaws of the cliffs, and empty...although his experienced eye was focused on the exact spot that the anchored ship had occupied the since the day before. Accompanying that image, mordant and incisive, tearing his soul, the reproaches of Hallet, now justified, presented themselves.

Abandoned without any other resource than a few days' food supplies that would be rapidly exhausted, what would become of them on these sterile rocks? They did not even offer a stream of drinkable water.

He had a second of frightful anxiety, sensing his intelligence vacillate at the breath of terror. The sun was going down. He thought that night falls rapidly, that in the dark, demoralization would not take long to take possession of his companions. And what reply could he give, if they questioned him? What could he offer to calm their fears? What hideous death had he not prepared for them by his lack of prudence, his stupid obstinacy in pressing ever forward into the unknown? On, Lina's joyful dreams...constructing puerile décors of precious stones in the cheerful morning light...!

By contrast, the faces of the sailors, congested by the rude effort of the climb and strewn with droplets of sweat, appeared at that moment, as if to make the horror of the situation more precise.

But their presence provoked a sudden reaction in Rogés. Another self stood up within him, and he listened to it speak with surprise. So much did his own speech seem to the lieutenant to be estranged from himself, from his preceding preoccupations.

"Well, my lads," he said. "It's higher than we thought, isn't it? A little break wouldn't be a bad thing..."

"To be sure," said one of the men, "especially as, with all this apparatus, it's not easy to go forward; and then, for us, land is...more inconvenient, you know!" He launched a jet of brown saliva and put down his tools.

In the meantime, his comrade had arranged the ropes in such a fashion as to form a seat, which he offered to the lieutenant.

"Thanks, my lad. Does one of you have my eyeglass?"

"Here it is, Lieutenant."

"I think," Rogés continued, confidently, addressing himself to Toby, "that this excursion won't have been futile. For although, unfortunately, I can't see any issue practicable for the *Dauphiné*, that observation will already have the effect of limiting the field of research to the northern part of the archipelago. As for us, I think we'll be able to return to the ship by a shorter route..."

He adjusted his binoculars

As he searched the slightest folds of the turbulent ground, continuing to speak in a simple and casual tone, developing what he wanted to set out in a clear and logical fashion that imposed confidence, deep down, he was frightened by so much duplicity.

"Yes," he concluded, "it's necessary to direct explorations to that side of the mountain. The sands that we encountered to port in the morning indicate, moreover, that there must be other low sections, and perhaps, among them, we'll discover the sufficient depth.

"In the meantime, a branch extends from the creek where the launch is moored, a thin arm that passes between these heights and goes to join up with the eastern pass, which we neglected. By that route, we'll cut our return journey short. We'll go around the foot of this plateau, around which the strait bends...

"Yes, we'll gain at least an hour, especially with the ebb-tide. The current will help us; we'll have the tide in our favor."

The two mariners understood, above all, that the immediate conditions of the return to the *Dauphiné* offered an agreeable perspective, by virtue of the shortening of the route, additionally combined with a favorable tide. Anticipating, moreover, that the chore was finished, in that they were not taking the ascension any higher, they expressed their contentment at each of the lieutenant's affirmations with simultaneous and identical approving nods of the head.

Toby, on the contrary, who had definitively lost the hope of encountering in that implicated relief map any indication susceptible of enlightening him, did not pay any attention to what Rogés was saying. The apprehensions that Hallet's early morning visit had caused to germinate in his mind were reborn, more forcefully now that the confession that had escaped the lieutenant before the arrival of the men seemed to confirm the imminence of a catastrophe.

The unfortunate Bob repented of having shared Hallet's ideas regarding the presumed flight of the general staff, ideas that he now recognized to be absurd. Why, too, had he provoked the confidences of the head waiter and forced Rogés' hand? He was irritated by

Hallet's stupid terror, his own stupidity, the blissful expressions of the sailors, wiping their suntanned and ruddy faces while listening to the lieutenant with evident pleasure...

As for Rogés, given that Toby was mistaken with regard to the real meaning of the young man's attitude, and did not suspect the anguish that was masked by the officer's calmness, his action in scanning the landscape with his binoculars and his tranquil tone irritated Bob terribly.

Time's passing, he thought. *Now, although, as Rogés says, his famous lobster claw might not be gripping the archipelago so tightly sealed that the steamer can't find an exit between two isles...what is that great devil of a plateau over there hiding? Who knows whether Laffite hasn't explored the northern part that the island is hiding from us, and discovered open sea? In any case, the ship has left its mooring. Where should we look for it?*

While that animal's perorating before his men, and tracing the shortest route to go...where?...the Dauphiné*'s doubtless in the process of heading for New York, without anyone being any more preoccupied with us than if we hadn't left... They're right, moreover, those people. Their delay is great enough, and it would be idiotic to burn the little coal they have left waiting for imbeciles who've gone on an excursion. In addition, we might have been lost this morning in the western pass. If they'd risked waiting for us any longer...and that's probably what they said to themselves...they thought we'd gone astray, probably, if not fled...*

However, we didn't hear any whistle-blasts, or the siren...

For a moment, Toby recovered hope, until he re-membered that although the steamer's funnels had re-sisted the mighty waves that had carried the bridge away, it had not been the same for the accessory pipes. The whistle and the siren no longer existed.

And to think, Toby thought, then, *that without that idiot Hallet, I'd be sitting tranquilly in the dining room now, in front of an iced glass, with the trepidation of days of good progress under my feet, instead of roasting here in the company of these brutes and their officer, waiting to suffer from hunger and thirst, and dying with no remission.*

Poor Bob!

One last time, the lieutenant had scrutinized, mi-nutely, the landscape gilded by the setting sun. Then he replaced the binoculars in their case, which he closed with a dry click, with the heel of his hand.

At that sound, Toby started and interrupted his re-flections on the treacheries of the past, the blackness of the present and the terrifying future.

He interrogated Rogés with a glance—who, while the sailors were occupies in picking up their unnecessary burdens, responded with a brief pantomime of despair.

They went back down, mouths dry, each carrying the weight of his thoughts, without exchanging a word.

The men, glad that the chore had finished thus, were singing while chewing their plugs of tobacco.

The one who was carrying the disks of fabric amused himself by way of a joke, sending signals toward the broad plateau supported by the mauve hills. He end-ed up, while tumbling down the slopes, by adding the word "understood" to the word "perceived," to the great joy of his comrade, whereupon the lieutenant displeased by the indiscipline rather than by the cheerfulness of the men, told them to stop that game.

When, almost without perceiving it, they had once again passed over the steps that they had scaled so slowly, they found themselves only separated by the final bank from the terrace of the lunch, overhanging the creek and the launch, Toby noticed that Hallet's pose was unmodified. La Pascalieri had improvised a *chaise longue* by bringing two chairs together, whose seats she had opposed. She seemed to be asleep on that narrow divan.

He also observed that Hallet was consulting his watch, mechanically.

He did the same, and saw that it was five-forty, half an hour later than the delay accorded to the lieutenant by Hallet to rejoin the steamer.

Toby immediately forgot his sinister preoccupations, the disappearance of the *Dauphiné* and the unreassuring consequences implied thereby, reconquered by the fever of expectation and the sentiment of an imminent danger. He did not succeed in warding off an instinctive fear of what was about to happen, recalling Hallet's decisive tone. Involuntarily, he constructed the scene in advance: Hallet getting to his feet, taking aim at the lieutenant, and pressing the trigger of the revolver. But he promised himself to get in front of Rogés and march at the head, in order to be able to disarm his comrade in time.

Nevertheless a frisson ran through him as he imagined the drama. He would have liked to slow the sailors down, who were, on the contrary, accelerating their pace, taking great strides.

The fatal moment arrived.

La Pascalieri, waking up, greeted the little troop with a smile.

Toby leapt down on to the terrace.

The lieutenant had already preceded him.

Hallet picked up his weapon. "You have another sixty-five minutes, Monsieur," he said, and put it back in his pocket.

Bewildered, Toby ran to the table and looked at the dial of Hallet's watch. The hands marked five past four. The watch had stopped—and Hallet, who had probably dozed off, had not noticed.

XI. The End of the Excursion

"Well?" La Pascalieri interrogated, yawning. "The ascension? Have you discovered a passage? When will we be in New York?"

Rogés replied: "We've only observed that if an issue exists, it isn't in this part of the archipelago."

"A fine result!" said the singer.

"On the other hand, we've discovered a new itinerary that will permit us to return to the bay quite rapidly. In three-quarters off an hour we'll be aboard."

That categorical affirmation caused Toby to start. He was occupied in concocting a toddy, in accordance with a delicate and complicated recipe that he liked. He almost dropped the spoon full of flaming liquid that he was carefully moving toward two sugar-cubes placed beneath, bathing in the cognac that filled a cup, disposed above a glass of water, constituted by the peel of two mandarin oranges whose contents had been carefully extracted, in such a fashion as to conserve, as far as possible, the spherical form of the fruit.

With great difficulty, Bob retained the composure necessary to the continuation of the delicate operation. Finally, the alcohol caught fire, and the contented himself with exhaling a bitter and ironic sigh.

Reassured by the lieutenant's words, which had demonstrated to him the impossibility of the *Dauphiné* having quit her moorings, but disappointed, on the other hand, by the certainty that suppressed any immediate chance of flight, Hallet addressed Toby in a reproachful tone: "It seems to me that you ought not to drink anything. You're going to delay us."

"You know, old man," said Toby, glad to let out his ill-humor, too long contained, "you're beginning to annoy me. Pack up the stuff in the meantime, if you wish. I'm in no hurry, myself. Not at all!"

Rogés, fearing that Bob was about to get carried away by excessively clear explanations, interrupted in a conciliatory fashion.

"Indeed, Monsieur Hallet—let your friend rest a little; the climb was hard. In any case, as soon as he's swallowed his toddy, my men will prepare the departure."

Hallet raised no further objection.

Groaning, because a gust of wind had just blown brutally, extinguishing his savant preparation prematurely. Toby bit ardently into the depths of his mandarin. The liquor flowed slowly, striping the water with transparent streaks, gradually communicating to it a color of burnt topaz, at the same time as an admirable bouquet of odorous fruit rose up.

After having distributed tasks to his men, Rogés chatted in a low voice with his mistress, whom he had taken on his knees.

Hallet stood up. So much sybaritism displeased him. He did not suspect that Toby, whom he saw slowly savoring his mixture, drinking in small sips, was thinking:

Stuffed—we're irremediably stuffed, that's certain. But if we're soon to resume, on our own account, the position of the castaways of the Medusa *on their raft, at least grant me permission to profit in peace from my last minutes of tranquility...the glass of rum for those condemned to death, what!*

For his part, the lieutenant, between two feverish kisses, could not extract himself from the obsession of the scarcely-witty caption of an engraving he had once seen in a humorous paper; it was imprinted before his eyes without him being able to chase it away.

Instead of the pretty face of the dancer, he imagined a roofer falling from the fifth floor, passing by an open window permitting him to see a young woman undressed, displaying very appetizing underwear, and he vaguely repeated the phrase that accompanied the drawing: *So far so good—as long as it lasts.*

Caught in the trap of his own assurance, he had to flirt with La Pascalieri, simulating a natural confidence, giving the usual orders, constraining himself to habitual gestures, and…in a few minutes, they would be ready to set forth!

And then….! An ironic haunting, stupid by dint of monotony, the refrain sang out again: *as long as it lasts!*

When they embarked, before taking her place at the rear, La Pascalieri remained standing for a moment, contemplating the cyclopean foundations, the shining peak and the circular haven already drowned in shadow.

"So we're quitting these parts, where no human has penetrated before us," she said, in a melancholy tone, "without bringing back either the precious stones of which I dreamed, or the vision of fantastic animals, or the humblest blade of grass…or, above all, the hope of cleaving the open sea again! Why have that mountain and those rocks emerged from the sea-bed, since they remain empty and disappointing? Perhaps people will live here someday though, and will have overrun these solitudes when we come back. Perhaps…I've lost the little amulet that I picked up this morning…in truth, nothing remains, nothing, except the memories…" After a pause, she added, not without a malicious wink: "And what memories!"

Those words stirred Rogés infinitely. Toby noticed it, and, fearful in his turn, for the lieutenant as much as himself, of a revelatory disturbance, he hastened to create a distraction.

"At least, Madame let's not forget any personal items...your cigarette case? No? And you, Hallet, do you have your umbrella, your handkerchief, your ill-humor? Yes. All's well, then. Row the galley!"

The launch quit the round creek and immediately engaged in the new arm that Rogés had discovered.

The channel formed a bed that went around the mountain, and presented enough width to allow the sails to be hoisted.

At the murmur of the water's friction, La Pascalieri, and then Hallet, sighed.

The men had resumed their posts in the bow.

Toby and the lieutenant looked at one another, without daring to express their thoughts otherwise.

And yet, with his benevolent cheerfulness surmounting al the proofs, and his indestructible optimism, Bob would have liked to comfort Rogés, whose despair was clearly decipherable now in the vertical wrinkles of his forehead, and his eyes, bright with fever beneath his furrowed eyebrows.

Poor fellow, he thought, forgetting his own fate. *He's obliged to take us to the mooring where it's certain we won't find the steamer, Now, in order to have raised anchor without us, it's evident that the Commandant of the* Dauphiné *must have been subject to the imperious pressure of circumstances. What could they have been? The discovery of a pass, or doubtless what he pinned up yesterday—the route rediscovered with the tide, and the immediate departure dictated by the necessity of not waiting for the channel to be definitively barred after a*

132

new elevation of the bed. So, little if any chance of ever getting back aboard...unless the ship stops outside the islands and ends someone to search for us...unless this land has been signaled, and other ships...a sailing ship...hmm...was sighted...

At any rate, that scarcely changes the present. Nightfall's approaching. How is Rogés going to get out of this shortly, with the men to whom he's lied, that fanatic Hallet, and his mistress, who'll only be able to criticize him and complain? A woman's caprice! He didn't know how to refuse... The insouciance of youth! The unknown attracted him... His comrade already killed himself, yesterday, for not having wanted to listen or see...

But just as Toby was about to communicate to the lieutenant the modest hope born of his reflections, and risk a few words of encouragement pronounced in a low voice, he perceived that the officer was tilting his head, that his hand was letting go of the tiller, and he realized that, after a sleepless night followed by a day of emotion such as that one had been, fatigue had become the best narcotic and the most efficacious consolation. Following the example of La Pascalieri and Hallet, Rogés was asleep.

That unexpected slumber, and the proximity of darkness, augmented the horror of the adventure tragically.

In spite of that, before the face of the sleeper, which had become calm and ingenuous again, Toby smiled silently...and took the tiller.

A sudden freshness traversed the warm air, announcing the advent of night. It approached in a robe of roseate brocade, with jonquil and amaranth decorations. Soon, its train of light floated over waters splashes with sumptuous patches. It occupied the vast plains of the

133

sky, whose bright sapphires died into amethysts in the orient, rubies in the occident, while on the land, mauve mists draped the distant horizons with their light sashes. The contours of nearer objects dissolved into imprecise, fluid lines; the number of visible details diminished; the night began to weave traps around the little boat that was sailing in isolation, lost in the archipelago.

The launch drew away from the mountain; its summit was plunged at present in a vault of pale sulfur, breached by fissures, with soft color ranging from turquoise blue to the milky green of dead stone, and patched toward the west with bloody streamers.

In front of him, Toby could still distinguish broader reflections, a kind of haven that the launch was approaching, a kind of vast intersection, a miniature interior sea, in which several straits terminated.

A residue of light glided over its polished metal surface, variously tinted in accordance with the depth, an immense golden plate clad with multiple patinas. Rocks cut out their silhouettes in somber plaques, opposing glaucous frissons to the ruddy waves, through which the flamboyant mirror appeared.

Insensible to the beauty of the décor, the magic of those magnificent waters, the enchantment of the sky and the strange aspects of the mountain, Robert Toby only considered the multiplicity of routes, and, recently alerted to his incapacity in matters of orientation, hesitated over the direction to take, all the more so as he was sufficiently acquainted with matters of navigation not to be unaware that a variation in the route requires a maneuver.

The lieutenant had said: "We'll veer over there, near that plateau, at the foot of which the strait bends."

Now, the strait, considerably broadened, split into numerous ramifications. Which one to choose? And the lieutenant was sleep...

Again, Toby smiled. Did he not know, himself, that none of those channels led toward the *Dauphiné*?

He abandoned himself to hazard...

Gradually, the immense golden plate that the boat was crossing was tarnished...the rocks of the shore were confounded with the nascent obscurity. The ruddy waves and glaucous marbles were extinguished. The mirror no longer reflected anything but a few errant clouds, and the first stars.

A sailor hoisted a searchlight on to the mizzen mast and attached colored lights to the frail steel shrouds. Hallet, La Pascalieri and Rogés did not wake up.

The breeze had weakened. The launch slowed down, and Toby looked at the sails anxiously; the flapping of the insufficiently inflated canvas increased in intensity. In fact, it did not take long to agitate the lieutenant, who opened his eyes and immediately sat up, taking the tiller again, after having shaken Toby's hand energetically.

"Thanks!" he said, quietly, and had the sheets tightened.

Shortly thereafter, the wind dropped further, and he ordered the sails to be taken in and the oars manned.

For those orders, involuntarily, he had given his voice curt and loud intonations that caused Hallet to sit up.

"Eh! What? It's dark...have we arrived?" he demanded, rubbing his eyes. "But...what time is it?"

La Pascalieri raised her heavy eyelids, and listened.

"Well, yes, said the lieutenant. "We've arrived, or very nearly. What's astonishing about that?"

Toby thought it as well to add: "What! You no longer recognize the bay? You're still asleep..."

"I'm still asleep!" replied Hallet. "I'm asleep? No, I'm no longer asleep, and what are you telling me about the bay? One can't make out anything in the darkness. Where's the ship?"

Uh oh! thought Toby. *This is where things get complicated. That's going to spoil things...*

"Where's the *Dauphiné*?" Hallet repeated.

The lieutenant did not reply.

La Pascalieri, who was still lying down, raised herself up on her elbow and looked. "Me neither," she said. "I can't make anything out."

"Are you sure, at least," Hallet went on, addressing Rogés, "that your new route hasn't led us astray, has really taken us to the *Dauphiné*'s mooring? We ought to have found her in three-quarters of an hour, and it seems to me..."

"What if I were mistaken?" the lieutenant interjected. "What would you do, if you please?"

Hallet, confused, bowed his head. "What do you mean...mistaken?" he stammered. "It's not true is it? You're certain...an officer like you, a lieutenant, damn it, doesn't make mistakes like hat. You're only joking, to frighten me...to frighten me, that's it! Just now, perhaps I offended you...I was stupid, boorish...I beg your pardon. Pardon me! But please...I'm a poor fellow...don't toy any longer with my fear. Tell me that you weren't mistaken!"

In spite of their platitude, Hallet's words translated such a sentiment of terror that Toby trembled, and La Pascalieri also became troubled. She leapt to her feet.

"In fact, Philippe, it's necessary not to joke about these things. Answer him!"

"I beg you, Monsieur Rogés," Hallet added.

Until then the men had been rowing impassively, laughing covertly at the passenger's anxieties. But the fear that veiled the timbre of Hallet's words had conferred on his final plea such an accent of anguish that at that moment, two of the sailors stopped rowing and turned round abruptly, sounding the darkness.

As Rogés prolonged his silence, Hallet could be heard weeping.

"It's true then!" sad La Pascalieri. "We're in the bay, and there's no more steamer! Perhaps you saw it leaving…bastard! Liar!"

Furious, she hurled herself at her lover, bruising her delicate fists, on which gemstones shone in the dark, on the metal buttons, embroidered anchors and stripes on the coarse cloth of his tunic, shouting in a hectic voice all the insults of her native language, furnished by her memories of childhood.

Toby, and then the sailors, interposed themselves.

It required the heavy hands of four robust men to contain the frail singer.

Finally, they wrapped her in a sail, which they were obliged to tie up and moor to a bench. They dared not gag her, though, and her stream of abuse, mingled with nervous sobs, accompanied by Hallet's moans, returned to the boat in sinister fashion, sent back by multiple echoes that doubled the horror.

By the faint light of the lantern suspended half way up the mast, they could see that the lieutenant, very pale, was having difficulty holding back two tears in the corners of his eyelids, and that his lips were trembling at each of the woman's howls.

Toby, overwhelmed, drew nearer to him and murmured, in a low voice: "Since we're lost anyway, what's the good of tiring out your men? Take advantage of the pretext that the night and his crisis offers us, to land and wait for daylight. We can improvise a tent with the sails..."

La Pascalieri had not shut up.

Rogés, his throat strangled by the claws of a terrible emotion, could not succeed in articulating a sound; his sealed lips refused to open. With a weary gesture, he accepted the solution proposed by Toby and immediately sought with his gaze for a favorable place to land. Beyond the rays of light projected by the lights of the boat, the extraordinary density of the darkness united the water and the shore in the same ocean of opaque shadow. Nevertheless, here and there, confused lines extending toward an inky sky, dotted that uniformly black sheet in places with rare tremulous gleams.

Again, Toby spoke: "Provided that we don't run into some reef as we approach the coast...can you see anything at all?"

At that moment, Rogés stood up with the abruptness of an automaton, his eyes staring, his body stiff, and leaned forward. Then he commanded: "Undo those cords. Lina! Lina, listen to me!"

She replied with further insults.

"It's ridiculous! They can hear you on the *Dauphiné*!"

Toby could not retain an exclamation: "The *Dauphiné*?" he said. He thought: *That's all we need. Now the lieutenant's gone mad!*

The officer went on: "Over there...its white light...we can't see any other because it's doubtless moored behind high rocks... To the oars, the rest of you! Come on, lads, pull hard!"

Toby explored the direction indicated, and only encountered a vague pale scintillation that was confounded with a constellation.

Meanwhile, the men were rowing vigorously; the blades of the oars were striking the water with a livelier cadence, a more violent impact. The singer, freed from her bonds, covered the lieutenant with passionate kisses, begging him to forget the recent scene. Hallet had ceased moaning and was shaking his head with a bewildered expression.

Before the rapid change of scene offered by the launch, Toby, who had thus far conserved a sometimes cheerful calm, sensed his reason reeling. A sudden vertigo hollowed out a gulf of anxiety in front of him, into which he slid miserably...

Why was he afraid?

It seemed to him that he was the victim of a nightmare, but the bad dream was going on too long! He gripped the side of the boat with both hands, possessed by the desire to lean backwards and slide into the water, in order that it should be over sooner, to be quit of those sailors marking their futile gestures with an obsessive rhythm, to flee the coward, the vain joy of the woman with the beautiful body...

He had already closed his eyes, when Rogés' last words sounded again in his ears...he remembered the telling detail...the white light! And he hung on to his life by that slender assemblage of words...

The white light! After all, the lieutenant was capable of recognizing a ship's light, where he, Toby, could not distinguish anything but those of the sky. A fervent hope unsealed the grip of his clenched fingers, colored the décor and its characters with more likeable nuances. Toby became the confident and happy man again.

He lit a cigar.

Then, by a disagreeable association of remembered images, as soon as the first puff, he clearly recalled the sight offered by the deck of the steamer the night before, when, with the steward and Hallet, they had no longer been able to find the smoking-room. The *Dauphiné* had been demasted since the accident... Thus, it was impossible to hang a beacon light any higher than the colored lanterns...

Either Rogés had lied, or he was mad, or he was steering toward a star...

While these deductions fooled one another in Toby, in the fashion of brief successive lightning-flashes that make the same landscape gradually more precise, illuminated more each time, the launch glided over the black water, lifted up by the regular effort of the oarsmen. At the rear, the lieutenant, in spite of the seductive proximity of La Pascalieri, did not turn his eyes toward the faint light that he had discovered, and toward which he was steering the boat in a straight line.

Suddenly, in the east, a bloody light emerged from the cliffs. Forms sprang from the shadow. The sea appeared, red with that light, and they saw that the launch had almost reached the strand opposite the channel from which it had emerged...

Neither on the edge of that beach nor along the nearby rocks did anything reveal the presence of a vessel.

Rogés gave the tiller a nervous twitch that directed the prow northwards.

The men accelerated their efforts on recognizing the land, and, seized by the strangeness of that race into the unknown. Toby forgot his fears and his reasoning.

With its passengers mute, guided by the breathless oarsmen who brought supple coppery sparkles from the waves at every stroke, the boat flew, clad in crimson, before the noise of the splashing waves, surrounded by mystery and solitude.

A promontory grew to starboard, while to port a new slope of the mountain gradually emerged from the darkness. A more precise light revealed curious appearances there.

The peak rose up massively, overhanging the void. Instead of the steps that Rogés and Toby had climbed on the other side, a frightful curve tapered away, plunging under the cliff, which was seemingly left without support.

Closer to the water, pale patches modulated the phantoms of edifices, which their reflections in the water of the strait prolonged in immense fluid architectures, swayed by the swell. The play of the reflections constructed facades, terraces and palaces massed under an obscure dome.

The launch moved along a wall of granite that took on the form of the long hooked beak of a bird of prey, sending back the sound of the oars in resounding echoes, and projecting an ample expanse of shadow over the sea. On the other bank, one could distinguish with increasing clarity the brightness of marble and porphyry, the fluting of colonnades, their capitals, the line of quays cut by sumptuous stairways, on the steps of which stood metal statues or empty pedestals. Plaques of gold gleamed on the frontons of temples. Varnished polychromatic tiles glistened, far beneath the vault. And beyond the sumptuous apparition, narrow black vessels appeared, bristling with masts, reminiscent of battalions in marching order, their long pikes raised, their insignia and standards rising up in the night, silently armed, enigmatic, awaiting a signal...

The sound of spurting springs, more distinct and more forceful, mingled with the murmur of the surf against the jetties. An odor analogous to the perfume of lust spread its warm spicy savor, its aromatic scent, its singular enchantment.

Once again, Hallet was the first to signal the mirage.

He looked at his companions, the somber cliff and the mysterious spectacle in turn.

"B...but," he stammered, "I don't recognize the bay. Am I dreaming? There's a city, ships at anchor. There are no such heights at the place where we left the *Dauphiné*. And then, all this...that noise...those odors...!"

"Come on," said Toby brutally, "what's upsetting you now?"

"Oh! He's telling the truth, you know?" exclaimed La Pascalieri. "A port! A port!"

The launch reached the extremity of the bird's beak.

"Don't all lean in the same direction like that!" cried the lieutenant, in an irritated voice, without any more reaction to Hallet's discovery, and to everyone's astonishment. "Look out!"

Under his energetic impulsion, the launch descried a sharp curve, and doubled the promontory behind which the marvelous phantasmagoria disappeared.

When La Pascalieri, whom the maneuver had surprised, and whom the rolling on the boat had thrown against Toby, got up from her fall, laughing, she thought she was suffering from a new illusion on seeing a sudden illumination ahead of the launch.

A few cables from the boat, in a profound fissure forming a sort of natural harbor, the imposing mass of the hull of the *Dauphiné* loomed up, its illuminated portholes spangling it with golden disks...

"The lieutenant was only half-mistaken, as you can see," Vincent Tricard said, at that point in his story. "His experienced eye had instinctively recognized, in that unusual light, one emanating from the beacon of a ship. Nevertheless, his mind had interpreted the discovery falsely, in attributing the gleam to that of a mizzen beacon, when a simple recourse to memory would have evoked the dismasted liner. And yet that error and that forgetfulness were fortunate! Toby accorded the larger part of it to chance, and maintained that Rogés had taken a star for a guide, thinking he could see the light of his ship. In fact, that has happened before. But Toby! And anyway, didn't he dream the whole story in the boat?"

"It seems, "I objected, "quite coherent, very long and perfectly logical. A hallucination remains without relation to the facts that precede and follow it, rarely lasts as long. A dream presents more absurdities, contradictions...in that regard, however, were did the murmurs of springs and forests come from, and how had the *Dauphiné* changed its mooring?"

"That's right!" said Vincent Tricard, and hastened to talk about something else.

I knew that it was necessary, with him, to refrain from asking questions again until it pleased him to respond. In any case, he had already told me a great deal that day. I didn't seek, therefore, to solve the enigma.

XII. Ports of Call

Although I've already mentioned it several times, I cannot insist too much on the disconnected fashion, interrupted by repetitions and long silences, and above all devoid of order, at least chronologically, in which the adventures of Robert Toby were confided to me by Vincent Tricard.

What I've reported of that story thus far dates, for the most part, from the commencement of our voyage, and our layover in Honolulu. The miraculous return of Lieutenant Rogés to the ship, when he had thought that the *Dauphiné* had departed, that extraordinary discovery of the new mooring, had in reality preceded, in my traveling companion's story, what you will be able to read later. On the other hand, it was in vain that I had tried in the saloon bar, thanks to Vincent Tricard's abominable drunkenness, to find out, in the end, how the officer had so marvelously rediscovered the steamer, and why the ship had quit her previous position without worrying about the absentees. I was only able to obtain a further development of the scene between Rogés and Hallet, drawing his revolver, and other anterior fragments then unknown to me, augmented by a few that you will know in due course.

If I come back to this point obstinately, it's because I'm now arriving at a passage in which I truly cannot separate from the frame in which the traveler of the Maison Loupe, of Bordeaux, exposed it to me, how much the décor and, more exactly, certain particularities of that décor, rendered clear to me the sentiments, emotions, thoughts, images and tendencies of the singular actors.

In spite of the care I am taking, before their relation, in the notation of the circumstances that aided me to understand them, they will risk appearing, I fear, when transcribed coldly, less intelligible than they were to me.

Perhaps I ought to have used these precautions already with regard to certain episodes—for instance, that of the western pass and that in which a scene of strange sexual perversion linked Rogés, Toby, Hallet and La Pascalieri. As for the latter, it was related to me at the same time as the one that follows. But there, although I deem it reckless to pronounce on the intrinsic value of new or unknown phenomena, however implausible they may seem, their lack of plausibility does not deny in any way the possibility of their real existence, the two series of aforementioned facts have nevertheless seemed to me, in spite of the precision of the narrator and the abundance of details to belong more to the domain of reverie or hallucination—collective on this occasion—than that of reality.

On the other hand, I am inclined to think that no complementary indication, such as invoking the intervention of troubles of the personality, can diminish its obscurity, for those to whom the explanation these events, such as I have summarily sketched them, appears insufficient. There, on the contrary—at least in my personal impression—the special atmosphere of the milieu in which Vincent Tricard and I found ourselves, adapted with so much propriety to that part of his story, that the latter acquired an evident enlightenment therefrom, and that at present, that part of the story no longer presents itself to my memory except with the accompaniment of memories that comment on it and clarify it. In reproducing it without them, I believe I would be cutting characters out of an old tapestry and applying them to a panel empty of the landscape, banners and captions by means of which the tableau in which they figured can alone be deciphered, and with which they form a whole, a harmonious ensemble.

Since the night in Honolulu, whether because he regretted having talked so much in the saloon bar, in the midst of the natives and the girls crowned with flowers, out of shame for his drunkenness, or for some other motive, Vincent Tricard had obstinately refused to satisfy my curiosity regarding his friend Robert Toby.

During the nine days that the *City of Rio* took to cross the distance that separates the Hawaiian islands from Japan, I could not, in spite of my reiterated attempts at seduction, succeed in bringing my companion back to the subject about which his first revelations had rendered me more desirous to know more. Veiled pleas, discreet allusions and direct interrogations all failed. My former auxiliaries, gin, whisky and cognac, were not successful this time; even the Manhattan cocktail had lost its influence. We scarcely talked about anything but the quotidian incidents of the navigation, and the common acquaintances we possessed in California, where I would return when my leave ran out, a contract linking me for another three years, in the capacity of engineer, to the mines of S***.

In Yokohama, I believed that I would never obtain the continuation of Robert Toby's bizarre adventures, for Vincent Tricard had to visit numerous clients in Japan and his affairs thus risked retaining him there for at least a fortnight, whereas, for my part, I had planned not to quit the American steamer until Hong Kong, in order to catch the mail boat there after having rendered a visit in the interval to a comrade who lived in Canton.

During the hours of the stopover, after which we were due to separate, he remaining on land and me leaving on the *City of Rio*, Vincent Tricard was charming. He piloted me round the city, which he knew very well, taking me from Sengenyama to Isezakicho, into the temples, over the bluff, to the market, and, after having dined with me, absolutely insisted on escorting me back to the ship.

When, the signal for departure having sounded, he went back alone the little steam-launch of his hotel, I couldn't help shouting to him, once the cordial adieux we had exchanged had been renewed at the gangplank: "And when will you give me news of Toby?"

He started to laugh. Then, as his boat pulled away into the thousand eddies and the clutter of lighters, junks, sampans and steamers that surrounded ours, he replied: "As soon as I have the pleasure of seeing you again."

"Really?"

"I promise. And I even..."

The rest of the sentence was lost in the hubbub of preparations for sailing.

The next day, a disagreeable surprise awaited me. During the night, one of the Chinese passengers in steerage had died, and when the medical vessel accosted us in the port of Kobé, the ship's doctor immediately had a long conversation with a little Japanese doctor with gold-rimmed spectacles, flanked by a colleague who remained as intractable as him. They were sustaining that it was a matter of a suspect case, if not the plague itself, and, as disdainful of the results of the autopsy as of our itinerary, inflicted ten days of quarantine upon us.

I began to regret, not without bitterness, on losing ten days of my leave like that, not having left the *City of*

Rio with Tricard, and having stupidly wanted to complete the voyage in a single journey all the way to Hong Kong, for fear of wasting fifty hours in Yokohama waiting for the next departure of a ship bound for Europe.

With my companions in misfortune, the poker players—they were going to Manila—and the ship's officers, I cursed the injudicious Chinaman and the "accursed yellow apes in the braided caps," as they called the Japanese doctors. But that exercise, entirely Platonic, only brought a mediocre consolation to our ennui.

On the tenth day, at about five o'clock in the afternoon, our liberation was signified to us after one last sanitary visit. At the same time, we were informed that the *City of Rio*, having not yet been able to disembark its merchandise, and, by reason of the long station, having to renew its supplies of fresh water and coal, and complete various provisionings, would not be effecting its departure until the night of the day after next.

A few moments later, as I was preparing to go down into the steam-launch that would take us ashore, I had the pleasure of perceiving a familiar face: Vincent Tricard was looking out for me.

"I heard about your misadventure," he shouted to me, as soon as he saw me. "At least you're well, my poor plague-victim?"

"As well as a man can be who's mortally bored."

He started laughing, and held out a hand to help me over the side of the boat.

"I've thought about that," he said, "and it's partly for that reason, having learned about the prolongation of your sojourn, that I came to look for you. My affairs have been concluded more rapidly than I would have thought, and in excellent conditions. I'm leaving tomorrow afternoon."

"With us?"

"Alas, no. I'm going directly to Australia on a local steamer. It's not too uncomfortable."

"I regret meeting you again like this and losing you again almost immediately."

"You're too kind, but don't regret anything— neither this separation nor, above all, your boredom aboard the *City of Rio*. The two of us are free, so, let's enjoy it to the utmost! I've prepared a little feast for you that will help you forget the miseries of the quarantine. To begin with, we'll go to dine in Kyoto; that will be a change from the shipboard cuisine."

"Kyoto?"

"Two hours by express. The train leaves at six. One stop at Osaka, and at eight-oh-eight we'll have arrived."

"But I..."

"You have your valise, since you were expecting to spend two nights at the hotel. Anyway, there's no need for a dinner jacket; I'm taking you to a restaurant in Maruyama that's hardly frequented by anyone except locals. It won't be service at little tables with pink lampshades, music and low-cut dresses...it'll be quite different—you'll see."

XIII. The Kiosk and the Garden

Through an open panel in the long low room where thin bronze candlesticks carried the high hesitant flames of candles, which was reflected from the pallor of latticework partitions, a minuscule garden was perceptible in the moonlight, blue and silver, with rockeries, dwarf trees, and dormant carp striping the still water of the pools with shadows.

To either side of the miniature park, the neighboring curved roofs, staged on the mountain-side, descended toward Kyoto.

A distant frisson of life, light and rumors rose from the city situated in the plain along the two banks of the river.

The bare room was gilded by the warm light that spread in sparkling paths over the flanks of perfume-burners, monsters and bronze vases, varnishing the mats and the paneling, breaking into brilliant fragments and flashes in reflections scattered over the tortoiseshell pins, black tresses, silk fabrics and broad belts of the women; outside, the cold, azure and white garden was fixed in an absolute rigidity of lines, its motionless contours surrounded by dark shadows. That violent contrast of tones, harmonious nevertheless, that ensemble of riches of exoticism, of mystery and of art submerged my soul under an avalanche of new sensations that poured a joyful intoxication into it, pleasant to yield to after emerging from the perpetual vision of the poor shipboard salons and the claustration in the monotonous harbor.

Within me, the exact notion of the real was veiled, and especially the ordinary proportions of the real, of its limits. I sought, without finding them, the habitual reference points, for no familiar sign any longer advertised the presence of the external world, the one that I had known before. So, I arrived at easily assimilating my impressions to the various images of a dream, so difficult did it become for me to believe that I had been able to effect that abrupt transformation of my recent evenings of ennui into that festival night. In place of the poker players and their unpleasant visages, the enchantment of powdered faces swaying above robes with heavy pleats. The ugliness of the furniture common to Europe and the two Americas had disappeared; no more velvet banquettes, no more tables with red cloths where my regrets had leaned their elbows...

Without seeking to understand, I feasted avidly on the beauty distributed in the double décor of the kiosk and the garden.

However, I believe that at certain moments I remembered once again the rapid course of the jinrishkas we had taken on our arrival; the falling night lit up by the lanterns of the little houses with wooden trellises; shadows, loquacious and laughing, draped in togas that equaled those of the heroes reproduced in ancient sculptures, crossing the paths of our runners. We had traversed a bridge, steep narrow streets, a park. Electric light bulbs illuminated a giant cherry-tree, and the porticoes of a temple.

Then...Vincent Tricard poured me saké and drank. The geishas sitting beside us reached the lacquered cups with precious and savant gestures, and there was laughter, salutations, and entire cheerful ceremony...

To the sound of voices, stringed instruments and double tambourines, maikos performed dances, whose pantomime my companion translated for me.

Afterwards there came the confused state I've just mentioned, the vertigo of the excessively immediate contrast, perhaps the influence of the warm liquor, sweet and slightly bitter. The painted lips of the musiciennes were confused with the red grapes bathing in the water of porcelain bowls, and I tasted a flavor of fresh fruit, without discerning its provenance exactly: grapes or mouth. Was it from brown bodies, sheathed in silk, mischievous faces, complicated coiffures, or from perfume-burners of bronze and scattered flowers that the irritating flood of perfumes emanated, mingled with the fumes of minuscule silver pipes and cigarettes? The garden became the background of a print, immutably colored with cerise and ultramarine, but why did the people in the foreground vary their attitudes incessantly?

Tricard drank a great deal; and was still drinking when he said: "Well, you haven't yet reminded me of my promise. That surprises me."

I confess that at that moment I sought in vain to remember what promise I had received from Vincent Tricard. Eventually, I found it. He had promised to make me forget the ennuis of my quarantine…and how admirably he had succeeded in that task. I had to respond to him: "All my thanks, my dear chap, you've kept it royally!"

For a few seconds, he was prey to a terrible crisis of hilarity.

His laughter found multiple echoes.

Around us, the black tresses, expertly combed, framed a quantity of faces with turned-up noses, rosy cheeks, creased eyes, shaken by the same gaiety by virtue of the simple spirit of imitation.

When Tricard had calmed down, he commenced by drinking—have I said that he was drinking hard that evening?—and when his cup was empty, he said: "What! You don't remember Bob now?"

"Ah! Robert Toby…that's true…as soon as we saw one another again…news of him, no?"

"And you're in no more of a hurry than that to know the continuation of the story?"

I sketched a vague gesture, which led my hand toward a bottle of saké. "No hurry at all," I said, pouring the liquor. "At this moment, I wouldn't cede my own adventure for all those of your Bob, for I'm living, not on a banal desert island, but a night some three thousand years ago, don't you know?

"Where are we, in fact, if not in the land of little brown men with shaven faces, citizens clad in robes and shod in sandals? I've seen them in the streets and in the public squares, them and their runners, their litters, their merchants! Now, what are they, pray, with their painted faces they shining eyes and their black tresses circled by golden cordlets? Recognize the dancers and the pantomimes, the players of citharas and tambourines!

"The adventures of your friend, Monsieur Vincent Tricard, I care about much less, in truth, than this miraculous resurrection, which at this moment I'm no longer very sure of not having reached just now in a trireme at a vanished port!"

I think now that the traveler for the Maison Loupe, of Bordeaux, can't have understood very clearly what I was expressing with so much vehemence.

Nevertheless, the disdain—sincere at that instant—that I affected with regard to Robert Toby's story disconcerted him. He had certainly expected, on the contrary, that I would show some insistence, and perhaps, in that case, he would have put me off until the next day, or shut up again. My attitude astonished him. He said, in an incredulous tone: "You're not interested in Bob? You?"

"Yes!" I said. "I want to enjoy this hour of olden days and I don't want anything more. Don't talk! And if the ornaments of this room, if these flames, these flowers, if these women, their dances and their songs, if this garden, if all this, in sum, is only a trick of my imagination, if I'm dreaming, let me! Don't wake me up! Do you want a drink?"

"Always!" he cried. "And I'm going you tell you the story regardless."

"No—I don't want anything other than the ballets and choirs of these figurines, surged forth from an ancient past. Their supple rhythms and their lascivious suggestions are sufficient for my ecstasy. They're brown, they're beautiful, they're ancient, do you understand? Ancient! Undoubtedly, they danced like this at the great festivals in Corinth, in Olympia..."

With the stubbornness of a drunkard, Vincent Tricard repeated: "I'm going to tell you the story!"

"Shut up!"

"I'm going to tell you the story!"

"Dreams are fragile and I'm holding on to this one. Tricard, my friend, I beg you...reflect! These women might have known Phryné!"

"I'm going to tell you the story..."

His obstinacy shook me. I thought aloud: "Dreams are also not without presenting some confusion...and why should it shock the logic of my present voyage into the past if my friend Vincent Tricard mingles a little more dream with my dream? Let these women rest! And amid their keeling slenderness, the baskets of fruit and cakes strewing the mats, the full cups, I'll gladly listen to your chatter, my traveling companion!"

The traveler of the Mason Loupe welcomed these words, no less incoherent than the previous ones, with a visible joy.

In time, alcohol didn't trouble in the least a surprising facility of elocution.

He began, therefore, and his story went on long into the night, only interrupted by a few libations and the caresses of my companions.

XIV. The Second Night in the Archipelago

"You're burning with desire," Vincent Tricard commenced, "to be informed as to the fashion in which the *Dauphiné* had changed her mooring. You're still burning, eh? Admit it!"

I didn't protest.

He continued, triumphantly: "Know, then, that the first boat sent out to reconnoiter the breakers had, a few hours after the departure of Hallet and Toby in the lieutenant's launch, had come back in great haste. Not only was there no question of the high tide, or a channel, but the soundings had registered, from one minute to the next, a disquieting and progressive diminution of the same depth: the elevation was continuing."

On board, during the absence of the boat, the fact had already been verified.

Having remained stationary until morning, the elevation, after that brief respite, had resumed a constant progress, which nevertheless remained exceedingly slow for the moment.

It was nonetheless necessary to get out of the bay, under pain of being definitively stuck by a beaching replete with dangerous consequences, for at any moment, an acceleration in that movement might be produced, and what would they do if the large basin ran dry?

The *Dauphiné* had in consequence raised anchor and had gone at low speed toward the other extremity of the bay, veering to starboard—which is to say, opposite to the direction that Rogés and his companions had followed earlier.

Before the banks of dried mud that extended before the rocks festooned with wrack, at the foot of the cliff closing the vast amphitheater, the steamer stopped and put a boat to sea once again. That one succeeded in discovering the eastern pass that the lieutenant had neglected, and in which the ship engaged for a long, difficult and scrupulous pilotage.

The steward related that odyssey at table.

"How many times," he said to Hallet and Toby, did we think that we'd stay, broken down, in the midst of those sticky expanses of mud and algae! The fear of being nailed in place by a new convulsion was clawing us…we were scarcely making progress…and perhaps we were taking so much trouble only to go into a cul-de-sac…"

"What about us?" asked Bob. "You weren't worried that we hadn't come back before you set sail, or about our absence from the bay?"

"Laffite," the steward replied, "hoped to find you again once we'd got through the channel."

"But after that?"

"After what?"

"After emerging from the pass, of course…"

"Come on, Monsieur Toby, you know very well that someone communicated with you the afternoon."

"What?" said Toby. "That's a bit stiff!"

Hallet looked at his companion suspiciously and said: "Aha! You were informed of the change of itinerary. You weren't unaware that we weren't returning to the bay. Why, then, did you keep silent when I begged the lieutenant to reassure us?"

Toby pushed away his plate and looked in turn at Hallet and the steward with astonished eyes.

"Come on! Is it the slightly extended excursion by boat that has tired me out too much? I can't understand exactly what you mean, both of you, by what you just said?"

"I repeat to you, Monsieur Toby," the steward replied, "that we communicated with you that afternoon—with you and Lieutenant Rogés. You accompanied him, did you not?"

"Yes, I accompanied him," Toby declared. "That's true."

"I will add, then," the steward continued, "that you were notified of the precise spot, recognized a few moments before, where we intended to moor."

"That's clear!" exclaimed Hallet.

"Clear enough, old man," Bob replied to Hallet. "I'm beginning to understand...where was my head? I remember now...I understand, but you...you can't understand. It's certain that we were informed that the *Dauphiné*..."

"Had been constrained to abandon the bay," continued the steward, "And that she was preparing to set off to anchor here."

"Exactly! By the way, remind me, I beg you, of the name of...the person who obligingly informed us?"

"What!" Hallet interjected. "You didn't get a better look at the person to whom you spoke?"

"Spoke...!" The steward smiled. "Not exactly, Monsieur Hallet. Spoke...at a distance!"

Hallet did not grasp the meaning of that rectification, whereas Toby, on the contrary, was increasingly sure of the truth.

In any case, the steward completed his explanations.

After having traversed the gully that slanted sharply to the east, but without reconnecting with the Ocean, the steamer had stopped in the shelter of the buttresses supporting a large plateau. Bob thought of the one that Rogés had pointed out to him, in the direction of the mauve hills.

Before pushing any further, the Commandant, desiring to spare his men, overwrought since the early morning by the repeated soundings, the difficult maneuvers through the banks and constant uncertainty, had taken advantage of the convenient observatory offered by the high ground to explore the horizon from there, instead of sending out boat again as a scout.

It was thus that he had, on the one hand, discovered the deep-water haven where she ship was presently secure, and on the other, perceived the mountain on which, through a telescope, the little group had been made out formed by Rogés and Toby, coming back down, preceded by two sailors.

They had then attempted to signal the change of mooring, and, from the peak, one of the men had replied: *Understood*.

Bob remembered the hilarity of the mariner sending signals to the mauve hills in the desert! And he realized that the signals had reached a destination that had not been foreseen by the sender, that they had arrived just at the right time to be mistaken for an expected reply, and to prove that the message sent had been received!

Toby did not insist, and the conversation soon changed course.

After dinner, during the customary evening stroll, in the company of Hallet, the steward and the doctor, Bob, who in remembering that day's events, felt a real pleasure in accomplishing that banal exercise and treading with contented feet the deck of the *Dauphiné*, did not take long to notice an unusual abundance of passengers. Undoubtedly the temperature, an exquisite warmth, had incited the majority of the habitués of the lounge to desert their customary meeting-place.

The nearby land, clearly illuminated by the moon, revealed a short distance from the motionless boat the long promontory that the lieutenant's launch had been obliged to double in order to rediscover the *Dauphiné*.

To the north, the bay extended toward distant beaches.

The relatively flat coast to the south and east presented vast miry plains and marshes.

At times, when a soft breeze, as warm as breath, blew from the west, it brought gusts of a singular perfume that Robert Toby could no longer breathe without remembering the strange scene of the afternoon on the mountain.

However, it seemed to him that the odor was not exactly the same, doubtless adulterated by those of the ship, although it still conserved its indefinable charm, and also a special power of mental deformation, whose effects did not take long to become manifest.

Hallet asked the steward: "Are the soundings in the northern part to be recommenced tomorrow?"

"I believe," the latter replied, "that I overheard Laffite talking about exploring that sector in the morning—the only one that remains unknown, since Lieutenant Rogés has traveled the west of the archipelago and we the south and east. But if we don't discover the indispensable strait and we're blockaded, I confess that, at present, I find myself getting used to the idea of no longer reaching New York aboard the *Dauphiné*."

Toby was surprised not to see Hallet protest immediately.

The doctor added: "It's very curious! In spite of the evident inhospitality of this land, its forbidding aspect, its aridity, the total absence of trees, animals and streams that one remarks here, I too am beginning to like this country, and I don't think I'm alone in that. All the signs of anxiety have disappeared. No one is any longer talking about the delay, the time lost, and the emigrants are already darting covetous glances at this virgin soil!"

"During our absence today, then," Bob specified, "A complete change has taken place—a revolution?"

"Well, yes," the doctor replied. "Optimism reigns, and even...something more..."

He did not analyze the contents of that "something" but Toby divined that it was a matter of impressions analogous to those to which the passengers of the launch had been subject on disembarking at the foot of the mountain.

As the strollers passed close to an assembly of cheerful talkers installed on disparate seats, the majority of which were empty crates garnished with cushions borrowed from the divans down below—for of course, along with the bridge, the rigging and the masts, the rattan *chaises longues* and wicker chairs had disappeared during the accident—a young man stood up and asked Bob: "Pardon me, Monsieur, but could you inform these demoiselles, who are very curious to know whether what is being reported is true? Did you not accompany Lieutenant Rogés in his exploration? And is it true, as the sailors claim, that you discovered, on the far side of that cliff, a city hidden under the peak that can be seen over there? Excuse me for being so indiscreet."

Bob recognized one of the young people whose gaiety had upset Hallet so much the day before.

The two groups fused.

Toby and Hallet, designated by the steward as having taken part in Lieutenant Rogés' expedition, had to defend themselves against an assault of questions, most of which they could not answer. The most detailed descriptions were expected of them. Hallet talked about quays, statues, motionless ships, and thus satisfied immediate curiosities. Nevertheless, Toby claimed that there was perhaps nothing in all that but the effect of a mirage.

In the course of the conversation, in which Miss Jane Slow participated, along with her sister Marjorie, their friend Jack Diver, a female friend, Dora Bowl and her brother William, who had questioned Bob as he passed, the two Americans launched into a discussion with the doctor of the possible existence of the city and the archeological value of such evidence.

Jack and Will attributed the entire archipelago to the fabulous Atlantis. The monuments designated by Hallet, and the inscriptions that one could not fail to find, were as many documents that would doubtless indicate whether it was necessary to attach the disappeared continent to the civilizations of Europe or those of America, to the Roman Empire or that of Mexico— unless they found that they belonged to a society equally foreign to both, and in that case, what revelations might surge forth from the prodigious discovery of rediscovered Atlantis!

They were enthused, calculating in advance the richness of the sepulchers and palaces, recalling their visits to Pompeii, evoking their recent memories of treasured admired in the museums of Italy, London and Paris.

Skeptical, the doctor attempted to moderate their youthful impetuosity. He sustained that Atlantis had only ever existed in the imagination of ancient geographers. The few lines of ancient authors that made reference to it were insufficient to define its exact location or size. Furthermore, even admitting that the Azores on the one hand, and the Antilles on the other were the summits of mountains belonged to a land submerged long ago, those points were too far distant from the latitude of the *Dauphiné* for it to be permissible to attribute the coasts they presently had before their eyes to the hypothetical Atlantis.

"In any case," the doctor said, "In spite of it being far from my mind to think that Monsieur Hallet has exaggerated, it isn't forbidden to suppose, as his companion Monsieur Toby, a witness to the same phenomenon, sustains, that he was duped by a trick of the light. Night easily transforms a bush into an animal; why should it not construct a city with rocks?"

"What about the statues, the ships, the gold plaques on the frontons of temples?" Jack objected.

"The imagination often adds to the illusions of the senses."

"However…the moon…!" said William Bowl, in his turn.

"…Was probably insufficient to illuminate the grotto—or rather the immense cliff—distinctly. In addition, I can't conceive very clearly the manner in which monuments of that sort were conceived intact after an immersion beneath the waves, preliminary earthquakes, I imagine, and finally, the formidable seismic disturbances that occasioned the gigantic waves of the other day. How, above all, are they localized in a single point of these islands? For we have not seen analogous vestiges any-where today..."

The conversation that the steward, Hallet and Toby had with the young women on the same subject took a much more lyrical turn. In the words of the Misses Slow and Dora Bowl, frequently repeated, like a leitmotiv, certain words and phrases recurred: *poetry, picturesque, the soul of things*... At times, the melancholy of the re-surgent vaults impressed them sadly, and then the glory of being admitted to contemplate imminently the evi-dence of such an ancient past intoxicated them, as the fumes of an excessively strong wine would have done.

Toby's reservations were insufficient to put a brake on the ardor that his interlocutors brought to their evoca-tions. Since the previous day, their enthusiasm for the archipelago whose marvelous birth they had admired had been increased by the enchantment of the climate, the magic of the perfumes and the vertigo emanating from the virgin solitudes.

That evening, the mere idea of a dead city, extended beneath the peak that they had been considering at length, religiously, illuminated flames of desire in their pupils and colored their faces. In those faces, pink in spite of the white reflections of the moon's rays, and those shining eyes, Bob thought he recognized a make-up already seen, sharp glimmers of which he knew the precise significance.

He was disquieted by such a similarity. Truly, the perfume induced excessively sensual memories.

That feminine babble troubled him...

A confused intuition warned him that these unwit-ting women were only indulging in puerile desires, pro-lix chatter and passionate gestures because they were transposing thereinto, perhaps unconsciously, other desires, other words and other attitudes...

And the image of La Pascalieri surged forth within him, and as it persisted from then on to double, irritating and mocking, the gracious and ingenuous silhouettes of the Misses Slow and Dora Bowl, Toby, after a short interval of that malaise, wanted to get away from it.

He was a simple man, who took no pleasure in that kind of perverse association.

He therefore drew away, under some pretext or other. Alone, he walked back and forth on the deck, still dazed, cursing the special warmth of the air and the malignity of the perfume. Then, continuing to recall the afternoon's events, he lit a cigar...and was glad to discover his mind liberated from any louche idea.

At a brisk pace, he went across the spardeck, animated by the noise of multiple conversations, more lively than usual. The doctor had not lied: optimism reigned, and even...something more!

In the course of his stroll, in fact, Toby observed the languid quality of feminine voices, the artificiality of bursts of laughter, the vibrant tone of replies.

The warm atmosphere, charged with the effluvia of the singular perfume, propagated a heady fervor, was provoking the awakening of torpid desires. In the fashion of a sudden light that strikes a steel blade in the darkness, transforming the gray metal into a sheaf of sparks, it was changing dull sensual covetousness, habitually enveloped in dissimulation and shame, into brightly flaring radiance.

From the rear he heard a song rearing the night with its heated melody; it was a chorus of emigrants.

Someone, leaning over the new balustrade that terminated the spardeck, was staring into the obscure depths from which the ardent harmony was rising. Bob thought that he could hear the unknown man modulating the passionate words in a low voice.

He drew nearer.

The young man turned round: a gentleman in a dazzling plastron, trenchant against the mat black of a dinner jacket.

That perfectly icy whiteness attracted Toby's gaze before he thought of raising it to the face of the music-lover; for, the supplement of the duration of the voyage having constrained the majority of the passengers to have recourse to the good offices of sailors, who are very mediocre bleachers, Bob thought: *By what miracle of skill has he succeeded in obtaining such a varnish?*

He was standing there in contemplation, preoccupied by the enigma, without being aware of the impertinence of his attitude, when the young man came toward him and said: "Decidedly, Monsieur Robert Toby, you can never remember the proverb...oh yes...the suit doesn't make...the gentleman!"

And as an exclamation of surprise was about to emerge from the nonplussed Bob's mouth, he added: "Shh! Above all, be discreet. I want to maintain my incognito. It permits me, as you saw this morning, to satisfy a few whims, and thanks to it, this evening, I've been able to spend a delightful hour here in the fresh air. Now that the temperature has risen, and the steamer remains motionless, staying in the cabin has become insupportable. I was stifling, and wanted to breathe a little—that's my excuse for this disguise."

In reality, La Pascalieri was lying. She adored changing sex in changing garments, counting among the number of rare women to whom travesty is devoid of ridicule, and knowing.

Different from the cabin boy with the mischievous, insouciant allure who had embarked on the lieutenant's launch, she conserved here the correct attitudes that befit her costume. There was the face of an adolescent with a mat complexion. The supple slim body and her narrow hips lent themselves marvelously to such a role. The pallor of the bare hands, and their aristocratic smallness, added a complement of elegance to the handsome silhouette.

Wonderstruck, Toby translated his ecstasy in an admiring babble.

After having accepted those compliments like a person who expects the inevitable homage due to her beauty, but is nevertheless not insensible to that homage, the singer went on: "Have you heard the news?"

"Everyone," Bob relied, "is informed of Hallet's discovery: the city…there, close by. It's all that anyone is talking about, and they're no longer worried about anything."

"There's something else."

"May one know what that other thing is?"

"Certainly. Those gentlemen, the Commandant, my friend and the other officers—the engineers, I suppose—have held a kind of council of war. Excuse me if that isn't the right term. It appears that they have scarcely any hope in the result of tomorrow's research, for Laffite affirms that the famous 'northern sector' appeared to him, from a bird's eye view, completely closed."

"Then…we're condemned to temporary, if not permanent, deportation to these deserted islands?"

"Oh, those gentlemen deem it inadmissible that we won't have been rescued three months from now. They're certain that we have food supplies in sufficiently large quantity for that length of time. Although we've stopped, as Philippe says, outside of our route and that of the steamships, he thinks that sailing ships are bound to pass by. In that regard, they're going to establish an observation post on the peak."

"I also think," Toby said, "that this land will be signaled. Perhaps, at this very moment, the newspapers are already commenting on the appearance of a volcanic archipelago in the middle of the Ocean—for, while we were adrift, it's not impossible that a long-hauler passing through the region has perceived, not all of its coasts, because we witnessed their elevation, but at least a few summits."

"Nevertheless," La Pascalieri went on, "they're thinking, in the case of the failure of tomorrow's exploration, as a precautionary measure, of disembarking the emigrants, their tools and their seeds. They'll cultivate the soil. It'll be amusing, won't it, if no one comes for a year, to play Robinson Crusoe?"

"Hum!" remarked Toby. "Robinson Crusoe was alone, or very nearly. Here, it will be much more complicated."

"Undoubtedly especially as...but I ought not to confide that to you...bah! And then, no, it's better for me to shut up..."

Bob shrugged his shoulders, and said to the singer: "You're right to remain silent. It's a very serious matter...and very dangerous..."

"What! Someone's told you! The steward, perhaps?"

"Neither the steward not the doctor, but do you think, then, that I don't know..."

"Certainly! You've launched a vague phrase to make me go on...well, my dear friend, I intend to be as diplomatic as you, and you won't learn anything if I don't consent to it!"

"Don't be annoyed, Madame, and answer me frankly..."

"No."

"How can we reach an understanding?" Toby exclaimed.

La Pascalieri, disarmed, deigned to smile and said: "If you're well informed speak."

Bob pointed a forefinger at the peak raising its rounded head beyond the cliff; then he sniffed the air and, this time indicating the deck of the ship to the young woman. Said: "*It* isn't reaching the ship intact, and what remains is combated by the on-board odors...fortunately. Deny, then, that it's a question of that!"

The singer bowed her head. "Yes," she said. "They're very annoyed that people are so occupied with the mountain and what it's hiding—city, mirage or empty cave—for they're afraid of people getting too close to it. They're certain that the perfume is in the soil of the mountain."

"Laffite knows, then?" said Toby. "And the others too?"

La Pascalieri did not reply.

A few moments before, the emigrants had fallen silent. On the deck, the groups were beginning to break up. In the place occupied a little while before by the circle of conversationalists he had quit, Bob could no longer distinguish anything but empty creates. On one of them, a forgotten blanket put a dark patch. They had gone below.

Fresh breezes passed through the atmosphere.

In the moonlight, the wrinkled sea was like quick-silver.

The sharply outlined coast circled its shifting light with shadow.

Suddenly, a tumult, like the gallop of distant squadrons, shook the hills with muffled rumbling. Then there were briefer sonorities: the crepitations of musket fire, irregular and precipitate detonations.

"Did you hear that?" said La Pascalieri, anxiously.

"Pooh!" Toby replied. "Some storm at sea."

"With such a sky, and without our seeing a single flash of lightning!"

"What would you like it to be? Anyway, it's already finished. There's no longer anything to hear."

"All the same," said the singer, "I'm utterly confused. That wasn't thunder rumbling, and those noises announce some fatal event—I have a presentiment...now, my sentiments have never deceived me. This morning, when I held the green amulet in my hands, it seemed to me that all peril had fled from me. Philippe laughed on seeing my looking amorously at that almost formless figurine. But I swear to you that I distinctly recognized the features of a little beloved sister, miraculously reencountered, which would have protected me efficaciously against all evil fates. I could have wept when I could no longer find it...and now..."

"It's necessary not to be so superstitious, Madame," said Robert Toby, swiftly.

"Oh, I'm certain that, in spite of your assurance, you must also dread some approaching danger—except that you're hiding your true thoughts from me, as men are accustomed to do, in order not to frighten women. Well, I'm doubtless nervous, but not cowardly. On the day of the accident, I wasn't afraid. I knew that I wouldn't die that day…tell me what those sounds are hiding!"

"I've told you."

"Monsieur Toby, I thought you were more sincere!"

At that moment, a formidable tremor shook the steamer. With a frightening rapidity, the prow off the ship plunged into a spray of foam, and the spardeck tilted to such an extent that several people fell over among the empty crates serving as seats and all the unfastened objects, which rolled in disarray.

In order to avoid an imminent fall, the singer and Toby were obliged to cling on vigorously to the balustrade, against which they had been leaning a moment before.

At the same time, La Pascalieri, admirably composed, said rapidly to Toby: "The boat's going to sink…we have to jump into the water as soon as it reaches us, to avoid the whirlpools, and swim to the shore…"

Dominating the howls of terror springing from everywhere, a piercing scream resounded nearby, coming from the stairway.

Toby, continuing to hold the iron rail in one hand, was able to slide along that far and pick up a young woman who had fainted.

Scarcely had he placed her between himself and La Pascalieri, who had hastened to come to his aid, than a frightful din split the air, followed by an abrupt shock that almost precipitated the three of them from the spardeck…

The *Dauphiné* resumed her normal equilibrium.

Almost immediately, the young woman opened her eyes,

La Pascalieri leaned over her. "You're not hurt, Mademoiselle? You're not in pain?"

She helped her to stand up. Toby recognized Dora Bowl.

The American woman, upright and confused, replied to the singer: "Oh, thank you very much, sir. Truly, no, apart from a slight pain in my knee and my right arm...bruises, probably...I don't even think I have a scratch...but without Mr. Toby, I believe my accident would have had graver consequences..."

Overexcited by the event, she explained: "I'd forgotten my plaid over there, and I was coming up to fetch it when that thing happened...I beg your pardon, sirs, for having..."

A nervous release overtook her. She hid her face in her hands and dissolved in tears.

"Calm down Mademoiselle, I beg you," said La Pascalieri. "Look—the sea is like a lake...there's no more danger. Monsieur Toby, couldn't you go look for something...a glass of water...cognac...?"

"No, no," said Miss Bowl. "Don't go to any more trouble on my account...it's...it's finished, I assure you!"

She smiled at La Pascalieri. "I'd like...," she went on, "I'd just like to go back to my cabin...one again, thank you, with all my heart, Monsieur, and you, Mr. Toby."

"Wait, Mademoiselle," said the latter. "I believe it might be better for you to stay with us for a moment longer..."

Bob gave that advice, although the presence of the singer embarrassed him slightly. But he thought that La Pascalieri's masculine attire would mislead the American woman as to the true identity of the obliging young woman, at whom she seemed to be looking with more benevolence than curiosity; and after all, the circumstances presented a character of gravity too immediate for Robert Toby to think about anything else.

He was confusedly fearful that further abnormal phenomena might occur. The increasing disorder, the coming and goings of the crew, the overlapping commands, curt and repetitive, alternating with whistle-blasts, impressed him unfavorably.

Bob therefore continued: "I'd like first, if you'll permit, to go for news and bring it back to you, in order not to leave you until you're completely reassured..."

Miss Bowl consented to that,

The footfalls of the anxious crowd and the hubbub of conversations animated the deck with the fever that Robert Toby had already shared on the day when the fruitless attempt to fit the rudder and the previous day, when the moving land had appeared.

It was not necessary for him to go very far to obtain information.

Ranks of passengers crowded around them designated the location of the three boats; they were about to be put to sea. Sailors were hurrying.

He advanced toward one of the groups, not understanding the reason for that maneuver.

The neighbors that he interrogated had already questioned the men, without success.

However, as the boat was lowered slowly by the lifting-tackle, a sailor, in response to a new demand from one of the spectators of the scene, turned round impatiently and pointed at the cliff. It was slowly approaching the ship, while seeming to flee northwards.

"We're going backwards," said the passenger.

The boat touched the water.

The mariner then explained: "Too right we're going backwards—and without the engine! The anchor-chain has broken at the level of the hawse-hole...and fortunately, otherwise we'd have capsized. We daren't drop another, on account of that blow...so we're drifting toward the coast, and the boilers aren't under pressure. Now, we're going to try towing her with the boats..."

At a whistle-blast from the crew-master he drew away.

Around Toby, people were making various comments on what the sailor had said.

What had happened? How had the enormous links of the chain been snapped? No undulation had creased the surface of the sea....

The force of the wind, which was pushing the steamer gently toward the granite wall, was far from equaling the fury of a hurricane!

No one could understand the new accident at all.

And then, would three boats, even carrying twenty oarsmen each, be sufficient to move the enormous mass of the *Dauphiné*?

Nevertheless, one might have thought that the rapid succession of dangers already run by that crowd had, in a sense, adapted them to the thought of danger itself, familiarizing them with it, with the result that this time, a relative calm had had no difficulty in being established, soon enlivened by jokes regarding the boats—"Let's go forward! Let's not go forward!"—and mocking challenges to destiny: "Thanks to these surprises, perhaps we'll soon find ourselves confronting a caravan coming overland from New York to meet us—unless a giant wave carries us to Long Island in one bound!"

The more moderate uttered the remark: "More than one unforeseen event never happens at the same time;

that game of seesaw followed by the rupture of the an-chor-chain will probably remain the evening's only inci-dent We can therefore sleep tranquilly..."

Incapable of discerning the frightful peril the ship was running, adrift so close to the coast, and despairing of receiving a clear explanation, Toby made the decision to return to Dora Bowl and La Pascalieri.

Beforehand, he looked in turn at the boats, the sea and the cliff.

The dimensions of the three boats remained ridicu-lously small in proportion to the mass of the steamer. They seemed like thin, frail black insects whose long multiple wings were agitating without attaining take-off sped. Disdainful and serene, the Ocean rocked them with a gentle swell, splashed with moonlight.

As for the granite wall, its appearance struck Toby with surprise.

It was looming up now, separated from the *Dauphiné* by about a cable, presenting on its vertical wall a very sensible difference of coloration, for at this distance such details could be distinguished quite clear-ly. Near the summit, the rock remained gray and full. Lower down, a deeper hue extended, uniform, varnished and...*damp!*

The last adjective that Bob pronounced instinctively clarified his thoughts. previously obscure and confused. They became ordered within him, furnishing him with the desired explanation. The cracks heard in the compa-ny of La Pascalieri certainly corresponded to a further seismic perturbation, in inconsequence of which the sea had swelled, rising abruptly to the level inscribed by the change of hue. The resistance of the anchor had initially imprinted on the vessel that exaggerated inclination, which risked sinking it prow-first. Then the chain had broken, saving the liner from being engulfed.

But how could the revelatory trace now be decipherable, except by courtesy of a reflux as sudden as the inverse flow had been prompt? And now the original level had been restored…?

Toby tried to establish points of comparison. Inexpert in such tasks, he was unable to recover any.

In addition, the wind was accumulating between the ship and the cliff, the spirals of dense black smoke that the funnels were recommencing to pour out excessively; they must be pushing the fires hard down below.

Impatient to communicate his discovery, Bob did not linger any longer. He forgot his previous resolution, which was to go back to the rear and rejoin Dora Bowl and La Pascalieri, in order to run to the "bridge."

On the other side of the rope, in the open space, Rogés, Santony, the chief engineer, and Laffite were talking animatedly.

Toby hailed a sailor of the watch, who consented to alert the lieutenant.

To Bob's first words, Rogés replied: "It's incomprehensible! These oscillations effected without any notable agitation of the liquid mass, without violent waves, without the classical effects of a tidal wave. At present, it's evident that the sea is lowering rapidly, below the level that Lafitte observed here. Is it the bed that's rising again? Is it something else? But what? In any case, no means of action! We won't achieve pressure for half an hour, and then Santony can't promise us a speed of more than three or four knots. For the moment, the boats are just about holding us in position. Fortunately, the breeze is weak, and if there's a current, it isn't drawing us toward the coast."

"You think we'll get out of it, then?" Toby said.

"I hope so, without daring to affirm it absolutely. The critical moment is certainly past, for, the anchor having not been released, if the chain had resisted for a few minutes more, we'd have been irredeemably doomed. At present, on condition that the depth doesn't diminish in an extravagant manner, we'll probably succeed in reaching the moment when the engines will function."

"And…afterwards?"

"Laffite intends to get out of this bay, in order not to be subjected to the beaching her feared this morning at the old mooring. We'll double the point near which we passed in the launch this evening. One there, we'll go northwards along the sound."

Toby thanked the officer, and, reassured, set off in the direction of the stern.

Near the staircase, the place where he had left Dora Bowl and La Pascalieri was now empty.

It was in vain that he went around the deck searching for then; he could not see either the elegant silhouette of the clubman-cum-singer or the bright blouse, short skirt and blonde hair of the American woman.

"Bah!" said Bob. "Miss Bowl will have wanted to go back to her cabin, finding my absence too long, and La Pascalieri, after having let her go, fearing for her incognito, has preferred to go down too."

He remembered, however, the strange gleam sharpening the gaze of La Pascalieri when he had quit the singer and the young woman.

XV. The City Under the Mountain

The wax candles with black wicks were sputtering.

In a bamboo cage suspended from the ceiling of the exterior gallery, a cicada, silent until then, began to sing.

A circle of slender figures surrounded me, attentively.

What could they understand of Vincent Tricard's speech, though?

Indefatigably, the traveler of the Maison Loupe, of Bordeaux, was still speaking in the midst of the light fog that extended before the porcelain faces, patches with a double pink disk of the cheekbones, before the hooded eyes, the laughing mouths, the smoke of little silver pipes and cigarettes.

He was speaking, and the scenes that he was describing became precise in my thoughts, superimposed on the décor, standing out with an almost hallucinatory clarity, so much did drunkenness confer a real eloquence on the southerner.

It seemed to me that on a night similar to the one that was lavishing its snowy clarity on the dormant garden, I was watching the departure of the *Dauphiné*, her slow flight from the creek in which she had nearly foundered.

At reduced speed, she went along the promontory in the form of an eagle's beak, and behind it, strands emerged plastered with moving reflections, to such an extent that when she was about to double the point and her prow was cutting through the silk of deeper waters more rapidly, the place where she had previously been anchored, at the foot of the granite wall, seemed to be occupied by an area of gray sand.

Of the entire bay, in fact, nothing any longer remained but a thin groove of liquid mercury, dammed in places by leaden beaches, and the cliff had visibly raised its arid mass toward the sky.

Finally, they reached the cape.

The mountain displayed its rounded peak, looming over the mysterious city that it sheltered.

No, Hallet had not been duped by a mirage. The quays extended in the moonlight, with their staircases guarded by a population of statues. The marvel of the colonnades supporting the golden roofs was clearly distinguishable, the architecture of temples and palaces, the entanglement of streets, squares and crossroads. One could have counted the vessels of the squadron lined up in the port, their masts and their antennae.

The *Dauphiné* drew closer.

Again, the mysterious noise that the passengers in the launch had heard, the sound of lively springs or quivering forests, spilled forth its rustlings and murmurs, like the appeal of invisible Sirens, and there was also the enchantment of waves of perfume, impregnating the atmosphere aboard the ship with their seductive effluvia.

On the "bridge," Laffite, transported, said to Rogés: "It's crazy! Everything here is becoming voluptuous: opening the eyes…breathing…the slightest sounds acquire an inexplicable charm…

"Oh, my friend, I no longer regret our anguishes, our efforts, and their lack of success, since they've brought us to this enchantment; and even if I have to pay with my life for such a spectacle, I'll estimate that it isn't paying too dearly."

The lieutenant replied: "Why do you want it to be thus?"

Laffite shook his head. "Why…? I don't know! But perhaps it would be better than seeing this marvel soiled one day by the frightful contact of our civilizations, the peak cased by a funicular railways, the monuments mutilated by imbecile tourists, tradesmen, and hotels implanted on this virgin soil!"

"Damn!" said Rogés. "You're jealous enough to give points to Othello!"

"Jealous?" Laffite repeated. "I'm trying to define what I feel, but I can't do it. It seems to me that words no longer have the same meaning here as elsewhere, that we're a long way away, as far as if we'd been removed to another planet, and believe me, I'd almost rather stay here forever. Do you understand what I'm describing so badly?"

"Yes," Rogés replied. "I understand it all the better because my impressions are analogous to yours. I know what the terms of which we're making use mean, but it would need new ones to express what we're feeling."

"Precisely! The correspondence between the verbal sign and the thing it's translating has be destroyed. Odors? That's inexact…these scents possess flesh, lips, a tangible existence! Music? No…those harmonies are embalmed and caressant and colored! City? We're looking at a deserted city? Get away! It's an unknown woman. She's asleep tonight. Nevertheless, we're perceiving the echo of her dreams, the reflection of her appeals, an entire language thought by that courtesan torpid beneath her heavy adornment of edifices, a language that moves us and attracts us, even though we can scarcely interpret it, and poorly! Perhaps tomorrow, it will ring more loudly in desire, more clearly, and perhaps we'll listen to it…

"Oh, hold on! One ends up enunciating absurdities in attempting analyses, and yet, we're enjoying such complex fashions..."

Laffite remained pensive, while Rogés stammered: "It was quite different, this afternoon..."

The singular emotion was propagated aboard, and everyone receiving the shock of those transposed sensations, multiple and novel, was as astonished as Laffite had just been. It was in vain that around the ship, the elevation, which had not been limited to the part of the archipelago quit by the *Dauphiné*, continued, that everywhere, the enemy land surrounded her, filling in a northward prolongation of the interior sea that the launch had traversed a few hours earlier, displaying in the south broad plains still damp and shiny, thus enclosing the steamer in the center of a large lake, and annihilating any hope of regaining the open sea. Those observations did not distress anyone. They were gazing avidly at the city!

Only a few of the passengers who were still on the deck noticed that the ship had stopped, moored by an anchor, and that the coast no longer presented any dissolution of apparent continuity.

They were not disturbed by it.

The prodigy of the marvelous city exercised a victorious domination that no one escaped.

In addition to that seduction captivating thoughts and enfevering hearts, the sight of the nearby jetties offering their refuge diminished the anxiety of the less brave, as if that unexpected port had been a rescue station.

Then, a cloud passed over the moon, initially veiling the globe of luminous alabaster, and then. thickening, plunged the mountain into a sea of darkness.

Cries and exclamations sprang up from the deck of the ship.

"Light! Light!"

"No, it's the moon…!"

"There's no more moon…!

"And we can distinguish everything, as well before!"

"They're lit up, of course!"

"By what?"

"Oh, it's extraordinary…!"

In a halo of pale light, draping the walls with brilliant vapors, designing in soft, floating lines and sparkling bands the ridges of constructions, the harbor wall, the contours of pilasters and the immobile vessels, the dead city extended, clad in a magical shroud of radiance. A kind of prodigal phosphorescence distributed its vacillating gleam over the edifices, its nacreous glimmers, but without the peak itself, which overhung the city, being separated from the surrounding shadow. Wan reflections crept over the waves, globules of a green-tinted fire that rolled in the hollows of the swell in incandescent emerald cabochons.

They came all the way to the *Dauphiné*; they attached themselves to faces, to garments, to the ropes, avoiding metal objects, which remained obscure. They impregnated the fabrics so profoundly that the glow could be transported to places opposite the source from which the radiations emanated, without losing their properties. Those effects were only destroyed very slowly. So young people had the idea of descending into the corridors, where they frightened a few cabin attendants by showing off their luminous forms, to the accompaniment of bursts of laughter, with the electric lights switched off.

Although the phenomenon did not engender any burning or scorching, or even a prickling of the skin, and did not present any dangerous character, it piqued curiosities so sharply, and provoked so many hypotheses, that many people wanted to be informed as to its nature, or at least its origin. Even the officers, troubled by the events that had succeeded one another without respite since the day before, were now under the influence of a permanent excitement, trying to react against the ambient nervous stimulation that was overtaking them, unable to defend themselves against the imperious need to know that possesses the mind imperiously before anything unexpected.

However, when a few first-class passengers asked Laffite to reassure everyone by sending someone to explore the mysterious city summarily, the Commandant had the strength to reply to them: "Certainly, Messieurs, I'm as desirous of knowing the cause of this curious phosphorescence as you can be; but nevertheless, I can't detach any boat or officer from the ship at the present moment, because we're not in any position to anticipate when and where the seismic perturbations might stop that have already, twice today, constraint us to change mooring

"On the one hand, in the case that the depth varies again, rising here and falling elsewhere, opening up a route for us, forcing us to set forth, the boat would be at risk of not being able to rally to the steamer, as almost happened to Monsieur Rogés this evening. On the other hand supposing that a cleft, an unexpected gap, chances to put us, at a given moment, in communication with the Ocean, it will be important to take advantage of it without delay, for you have witnessed the rapidity with which, yesterday, the inverse event occurred."

"However, Commandant," one of the delegates replied, "what intrigues us might perhaps constitute an indication revealing the presence out there of living beings, hostile or friendly." He hastened to add: "I'm not unaware that that supposition seems scarcely admissible, but my God, two days ago, a hypothesis situating land, mountains and a city in this region would scarcely have seemed less implausible!

"Other people think that these lights, as well as the odorous emanations that are troubling us, making us uncomfortable, and the excessive heat of the air, must come from a volcanic crater located behind the city. Undoubtedly sulfurous vapors would be more convincing, and redder glows too. Who can affirm, though, that we're not at the mercy of a sudden explosion, an eruption, and an inundation of lava?"

"Would you want me to expose my men to that, then?" asked Laffite. "It seems to me, moreover, that the distance separating us from that hypothetical crater constitutes a sufficient guarantee."

"Finally, Commandant, don't you fear that our uncertainty with regard to that city—for doubt is no longer permissible; those are not blocks of rock simulating human works—and the various fluids that it's projecting might constitute a danger in themselves?"

"Obviously, Monsieur," Laffite replied, cutting short all discussion, "it would be very interesting to be informed immediately, and believe me, I would like nothing better than to satisfy a very legitimate curiosity, to which I do not remain a stranger; but first of all, I don't believe that an immediate exploration offers any utility whatsoever from a point of view other than scientific or archeological, and that our security would gain nothing by it; furthermore, I repeat, it is absolutely forbidden to me by circumstances to attempt a reconnaissance of that sort. I regret it infinitely, Monsieur, I assure you. Tomorrow…we'll see!"

Toby, who was prowling around there, witnessed that conversation. Then, when the passengers had gone, he heard Laffite ask of Rogés: "Living beings? A volcano? What do you think?"

"Oh, as for me," the lieutenant replied, "I'm beginning not to know what to think. I'm dazed and stunned, incapable of putting two reasonable ideas together. If one of those longboats immobile over there, equipped, came to range alongside the *Dauphiné*, and specters descended from it to invade the deck…that would appear to me to be quite natural and simple! For the moment, I only believe that I'm already dreaming!"

"That's true, my poor Rogés," said Lafitte. "You must be horribly tired. Go and get some sleep—go on!"

Bob, certain then that no one would be going ashore that night, did not listen to any more, and, being weary himself, set off to return to his cabin.

At the bottom of the first-class stairway, occupied in watching the play of the little green flames, which sowed his hands and the fabric of his garment with luminous vapors, and were only fading away slowly, he distractedly followed the starboard corridor instead of taking the port one, which led to his cabin.

He did not begin to suspect his error until the moment when, standing before a door placed at the distance he was habituated to cross, he read the number inscribed on the lintel mechanically, and did not find his own in the numbers painted there.

During the moment of hesitation that retained him then, the door-catch clicked.

Toby heard the sound of kisses. Someone emerged, with their back turned to him, and then turned round, and, having perceived him, did not manifest any embarrassment.

Bob recognized Dora Bowl, and, through the gap in the doorway, La Pascalieri...

Without admitting it to himself, Toby loved the singer and had thought her, very naively, an "honest man"—for Toby, it appears, cherished those sorts of illusions, and his optimistic nature refused to attribute malignity willingly to individuals, as to events. On this occasion, being unable to doubt the identity of the individuals, he would at another time have been heartbroken by the perfidy of hazard. Doubtless he would have criticized by turns the fatal desire to seek information that had taken him away from the young woman, his overly great confidence in La Pascalieri, and the insidious charm of the intoxicating perfume disturbing hearts and minds. Then he might perhaps have convinced himself that it was only, in sum, a joke on the part of the singer, having desired to test on the young American woman the power of seduction that the masculine attire conferred on her adolescent face, and ready to divert her success to scorn.

At least, Bob knew very well that Robert Toby would have thought so a week earlier. But at the same time, he was astonished that those judgments, that fashion of envisaging the incident, only presented itself to his mind with a quasi-retrospective, cold, unemotional character—produced, in a way, by the force of habit—while an entirely different sentiment led him to consider the event inversely, by simultaneously admitting the misdemeanor as perfectly proven and its authors not guilty...and those very words—*misdemeanor, guilty*—

rolled in his mind like empty forms, fleshless skeletons. Their physiognomy became foreign to him.

He understood then, vaguely, that the disturbance felt on the deck in the evening, the delirium confusing various, heterogenous sensation, amalgamating them in complex and new impressions, also extended to the domain of sentiments and ideas. He remembered the silence that the actors in the strange scene that had taken place on the mountain had maintained with regard to one another. No one had emitted words of criticism or approval...

Here, it was the same.

Dora Bowl retained, in the scatter of her blonde hair, a pure, smiling face of frank pleasure, with no trace of cynicism or effrontery.

In that regard, Vincent Tricard reported what Robert Toby said:

"It was no longer a matter of virtue or vice. Amorous and pretty...that was what had meaning.

"Oh, I believe that in confrontation with that damned enchanted city we had become, from the Commandant all the way to the least of scullions, true sages, philosophers such as there have never been elsewhere. And simply, you see, Vincent, because we found ourselves drunk...oh, not on drink, but on perfume, on music, on light, on a heap of marvels...and just as a drunken man can no longer lie, we were constrained to the truth.

"Until that moment, the women were lying in refusing themselves, and the men were lying in seeming to believe them...and anyway, all of civilization and all morality—what a lie! What an infinity of lies! And I think that alone causes evil, that it makes people remain miserable and anxious, occupied with a thousand imbecile quarrels! They take those lies for truths, those words for things…while out there, scrubbed clean of that filth of errors, we knew more than happiness…real life!

"Of course. I didn't reflect on all that at the time. I was just content to sense my mind free and clean, and finally capable of looking at everything solely from the reasonable point of view.

"I remember thinking: *How has that not been perceived already?*

"Thus, one admits that it's necessary to be a child to strike or insult an item of furniture into which one has bumped; one doesn't think of demanding benevolence or virtue from a chair; and yet, an individual is no any more capable on his own of changing the size of his skull by an inch, or the color of his ideas by a nuance, than a chair can shorten its arms of its own accord, or modify the dye of the fabric that covers it!

"And I wish you could have seen that little Miss Bowl not stopping for me, kissing La Pascalieri frankly, and that it was only beautiful to see such a thing...but no! You'd laugh, you! You haven't confronted the city under the mountain...you're still filthy..."

How simple that story, vivified by Vincent Tricard's loquacity and his eloquent drunkenness, seemed to me, how admirable and not at all dirty, out there in Kyoto, between the double gold and silver clarity of wax candles and the moon, in the warm atmosphere embalmed with strong and delightful scents, in the middle of bowls of fruit and cups strewing the white mats, near supple slender brown bodies draped in marvelous silks and crowned with pale, painted, curious smiling faces!

In the same way, the entire end of that extraordinary narration, having treated the sojourn of about a month that the passengers of the *Dauphiné* made in the archipelago, seemed to me, on that night and in that décor, easily comprehensible and even particularly limpid. On rereading the brief notes made the day after those confidences, I perceive that the life of that group thrown into such disconcerting conditions of existence remains as difficult to imagine as it is to describe, in spite of the precision of certain parts of Vincent Tricard's discourse.

In order to remain as clear as possible, therefore, I shall first extract from the complex descriptions reported by the traveler for the Maison Loupe, of Bordeaux, the relation of the material conditions in which Toby and his companions found themselves, and then I shall try to reproduce the indications relating to the strange mental state of those people.

XVI. The Four Cities

As soon as they had acquired the certainty that, all the issues having been sealed by the latest elevation, the *Dauphiné* could no longer quit the salty lake where she was anchored, in the absence of an upheaval that the calm that followed the preceding events did not permit the expectation, the plan settled upon by the general staff of the ship, which La Pascalieri had summarily explained to Robert Toby, was executed. An observation post was installed on the heights of the peak; it was provided with apparatus that would permit it to communicate efficaciously with the open sea and the steamer. The archipelago was explored minutely, almost all of which islets had been connected up as a consequence of the second elevation, henceforth to form no more than two unequal territories separated by the western pass, which now terminated in a narrow channel hollowed out through beaches of sand.

Those operations required about a week, after which the steward proceeded with the division of the cultivable land between the emigrants. Access to the city was then accorded to the passengers.

It was immediately perceived that the city, very large, and which must once have contained a large population, had been constructed under the mountain in a cavern, whether real or artificial, they could not determine. The vault of that immense grotto was, in fact, formed of a kind of armor plating composed of sheets of gold so cleverly assembled that one could not discover either joints or rivets there, and it was reminiscent of a gigantic breastplate forged in a single piece.

By what method had such a marvel been realized?

How had such solidity, and such a strength of resistance, not appropriate to that metal, been obtained?

Was it really gold?

In what fashion could a people live thus, and the city receive sufficient aeration?

They were as many points on which Vincent Tricard omitted to furnish me with the slightest clarification.

However, that particular disposition of the city explained its state of conservation, at least for the part situated under the mountain. As for the rest, this is what the traveler of the Maison Loupe, of Bordeaux, called, after Robert Toby, "the doctor's explanations."

The latter supposed that after the initial catastrophe, the city must have been situated at the edge of a bay, either circular and only communicating with the sea by means of a narrow bottleneck, or elongated and tapering in the direction of the Ocean, and additionally surrounded by mountains whose height surpassed in measure the greatest dimension of that natural port,

As no human skeleton, no mummified body, no bone subsisted, either in the streets or in the dwellings, he imagined that one, and perhaps several earthquakes before the definitive cataclysm, obstructing the pass, had terrified the inhabitants, leading them to flee their homes, to abandon their useless vessels and the region that had become dangerous.

It is thus understandable that when the continent was swallowed up, the sudden flood, impotent against the broad base of such a dyke entirely circling the port and the city, had only had the effect of compressing the cliff of those walls of rock, which was circular or oval, until it formed a kind of lid under which a part of the harbor and the entire city were sheltered.

That conception, evidently, was inspired by the banal observation of analogous facts frequently seen with regard to collapses burying workers alive and without wounds.

According to the same hypothesis, when the recent convulsion had wrenched that fragment of Atlantis from the abyss, the heaped up earth and blocks of granite had crumbled away from one side to the other as soon as the formidable pressure of the waters and ceased to keep them piled up. They had opened like the edges of a poorly-scarred wound from which the bandage is removed. Only the peak subsisted, doubtless thanks to its interior armature, its armor-plating of gold plaques.

In that regard, it was observed that the vault of metal had been constructed with a double objective: to oppose the possible collapse of the mountain and to collect the filtrations of subterranean waters, for the oozing of the walls of a grotto alone, even one as vast as that one, would not have been able to aliment the vast reservoirs that were discovered in various places, from which departed a complex network of channels.

The aqueducts, however no longer presented any trace of liquid, either because a preliminary barrage had dried out the principal conduits or because the catastrophe had inverted the order of layers of permeable earth in the bosom of the peak. They had been invaded by an abundant vegetation of lichens and mosses, dead for a long time, which nevertheless still nourished legions of curious insects, the only living beings that the archipelago contained.

The noise of springs first perceived by the passengers of the launch and afterwards by those of the *Dauphiné*, did not come from there.

It had struck the visitors to the city as soon as they entered it.

"Instead of the lugubrious silence of a necropolis," Miss Jane Slow had said to the little group of her usual companions, augmented by Robert Toby and Hallet, "there are songs and cries, a whole concert that gives the illusion of life in a magical city!"

"Perhaps it really is inhabited?" hazarded Jack Diver.

"It's true," said Miss Jane, "that instead of the slightly fearful respect inspired by mute tombs, once experiences something akin to an impression of welcome."

"Listen carefully," said William Bowl, in his turn. "One might think that it's the very steps of the stairways, the domes of the palaces and the columns of the temples that are saluting us..."

"He's right," Toby confirmed, after having lent an ear to it.

The little troop stopped before a sumptuous edifice decorated by polychromatic friezes that unfurled without interruption, for the monument revealed no door or window.

Further on, streets plunged under the mountain with the golden sky toward profundities illuminates by the lunar clarity, the singular phosphorescence that could not be seen overflowing in milky waves from jade corbels deposited at irregular intervals.

The sonorous frisson continued...

It was a very agreeable sound, composed of crystalline murmurs, of more muted sounds, susurrations, gurgles, rustlings and multiple echoes, resonances disconcerting by virtue of their multiplicity and their persistence. It emanated from everywhere, without anyone knowing to what it might be attributable.

However, it happened that Toby, having noticed, not far away, on the agate flagstones that paved the ground, a plate of sculpted metal doubtless fallen from a fronton, asked the two Americans to help him lift it up.

When they had placed it upright against the wall of a temple, they distinguished, engraved in a broad manner, with enamel reliefs, individuals in loose garments sitting around a table cluttered with cups and various utensils.

As the friezes of the palace did not bear any motifs of decoration reproducing human figures, plants or animals, Toby's discovery interested his companions keenly.

Appreciations overlapped;

"That resembles certain Byzantine metalwork," said William Bowl.

"A banquet! So these people ate and drank!" said Marjorie.

"With their annealed beards and high foreheads, they have the air of Assyrian monarchs," observed Jack Diver.

"I'm disappointed," confessed Miss Slow.

"Why, Mademoiselle?" asked Hallet.

"Because you all sicken me! Yes, this work resembled Byzantine enamels. Yes these people eating and drinking have the heads of Assyrians...and I would so much have liked..."

"...Them to have wings and fantastic attributes!" Marjorie put in.

"Silly!"

"No! I'd hoped that their strange light, that miracle offered by their port, and its vessels, and its statues, perhaps only represented an animal race, placed on the threshold of the city as we sculpt lions or bulls in the middle of our parks, but subservient to a superior people, dominated by creatures more divine than human..."

"Console yourself, Mademoiselle," said Toby then, "for these people were diabolically more astonishing than us, if I can judge by their music."

"What's that? Their music?" Jack interrogated.

"Yes, I believe I've divined its secret."

"Oh, do tell! Speak!" cried the entire group.

"The wall has fallen silent," Bob replied, simply.

"What yarn are you spinning?" grumbled Hallet. "Explain yourself! You're always talking in enigmas."

"I understand!" exclaimed William Bowl. "I understand! It's the light that doesn't traverse the metal plate!"

The young women burst out laughing, and Dora said to her brother: "Well, Will, personally, I don't understand at all. Monsieur Toby said the wall isn't talking any more, and you said it's the light. What does that mean?"

The young man explained then. "It's the ornaments encrusted in these walls that really emit the various sounds that we can hear. Look—these different emblems are composed of sheets of a thin and iridescent substance, stuck together and thus imprisoning liquids, probably sensitive to the radiations of the singular fluid that illuminates the city and projects its phosphorescence all the way to the ship...

"In addition, metallic sheaths, fixed at different heights, form screens by means of which the condensation of vapors produced down below is accomplished, in such a way that each sign furnishes the monotonous song of a minuscule kettle exposed to a perpetual fire, But here, in his part covered by the shadow of the sculpted plaque, there, where we've just placed it, the wall has indeed fallen silent, as Monsieur Toby says, because that light doesn't traverse the metal."

"Why that complication of ornaments that sing?" asked Marjorie.

William Bowl reflected for a moment, and then said: "It must be a matter of a kind of writing, addressed simultaneously to the eye and the ear: speaking signs, double hieroglyphs…"

"In that case," Miss Slow exclaimed, "they decipher themselves..."

"Not entirely! We can, however, try to decipher them."

William Bowl's hypothesis was correct, and the day after that discovery, after having exerted their attention to distinguish the successive sounds of a group of inscriptions, the passengers of the *Dauphiné* succeeded quite rapidly in giving the principal monuments their names of old. The only difficulty resided in that the emission, simultaneous and continuous, of those various sounds rendered their audition confused to begin with.

As for the substance that produced such effects, the caloric and illuminating power of which had not been weakened by the centuries, they were unable to identify it, lacking the instruments necessary for a serious analysis.

For myself, I suppose that the substance must belong to the family of the recently isolated radium, which has analogous properties, at least with regard to the permanence of the emission of luminous vibrations.

They found it in great abundance in the jade corbels of the public thoroughfares and elsewhere, in the firm of small rods and powder.

They made use of it aboard the steamer, its usage presenting no inconvenience. They could, however, one transport it by means of metallic instruments: tongs, spoons, or others. Picked up directly, or even through a fabric, it caused intense burns, accompanied by a redness that extended throughout the afflicted limb.

That was the only mode of lighting in the city—or, rather, cities, for the city was divided into four quarters, each forming a unit distinct from its neighbor, as much by the nature and destination of its edifices as by the materials employed in their construction.

There was Fu-twa-tçi, a name repeated by all the palaces and the temples facing the sea, by the pedestals of the statues and the stones of the pier, the city of material life.

Under the mountain, separated from the first by walls of basalt, porphyry and onyx, extended, to the right of a wide boulevard, Çri-twa-tçi, the city of intelligent life, all of metal, and to the left, Rhâ-twa-tçi, the city of the diminished life, a city of wood and papyrus, almost entirely destroyed.

At the extremity of the avenue, very far away, stairways led to staged terraces splitting the golden vault, and, isolated from the other three cities, dazzling with light, embalmed like a marvelous cassolette, Tim-tçi, the city of pleasure, slept, voluptuous still in the scatter of its brilliant fabrics, scarcely faded, its villas of painted silk, with lintels on which the names sounded as cheerfully as birdsong.

In none of the first three cities was any trace found of individual habitations. Everywhere, on the contrary, the same disposition was found: dormitories, refectories and swimming baths, indicating a communism that, in our civilizations, has scarcely been realized thus far except in fragmentary form, by boarding schools, convents, barracks and prisons. In addition, the absence of private storerooms, workshops and instruments of labor indicated a particular mode of division of manufactured objects, and the attribution of production to another location on the continent, or perhaps a fifth part of the city.

In spite of the magnificence of its appearance and the richness of its monuments, Fu-twa-tçi, of the sumptuous facades reflected by the waves, only constituted in reality a vast agglomeration of docks and warehouses; its palaces and temples served uniquely to shelter various kinds of merchandise, as the passengers of the *Dauphiné* were able to convince themselves on the day when it was perceived, by chance, that the superb colonnades dissimilated, inside their marble and porphyry shafts, a complicated system of chains and counterweights. The mechanism, when triggered, raised up over the quays, from the depths of the water to the height of the roofs of the edifices, large cradles of a yellow metal, analogous to the one composing the giant vault but lighter than aluminum, which had not been oxidized by its sojourn beneath the sea.

Gradually, they understood that these cradles were destined to receive the vessels and their cargoes, for the examination of the long black ships showed that their holds consisted of two large mobile frames, one placed at the front and the other at the rear, internally subdivided into smaller compartments, the whole interchangeable and able to slide very easily outside the flanks of the vessel all the way to the superior halls, operated by the receive—which permitted an extremely rapid mode of unloading. Inside the halls, those frames, only containing objects of the same kind, were arranged as they arrived. The edifices themselves were specialized; thus, there were the various warehouses of foodstuffs, garments, etc...

In places, their contents were almost entirely reduced to the condition of various dusts, among which only a few seeds here, a few shreds of fabric or fur there, permitted the reconstitution of the nature of the residue. However, the warehouses of metals and that of jewels offered marvelous collections, only depreciated by a few items corroded by rust.

From Fu-twa-tçi, a complex network of distribution tubes and vast subterranean corridors extended toward the other cities, embodying various means of communication. The means of transportation used there, in addition to differences in levels, by the artifice of something like roller-coasters—which explained the necessity of raising the provisions in bulk to the summits of the edifices—included various machines of which the *Dauphiné*'s engineers were unable to discover either the principle or the operation.

Santony and his lieutenants were equally disconcerted when, having crossed the basalt enclosure, they penetrated, in Çri-twa-tçi, into one of the numerous halls that must have served simultaneously as schools, libraries and laboratories. They encountered there, among debris of every species, a few sets of apparatus that had remained intact, which rendered them as stupid as a central African tribesman would have been before a dynamo or a Leyden jar.

The doctor, more fortunate, succeeded in discerning steam-baths and an ingenious apparatus based—insofar as the data furnished by Vincent Tricard, according to what Toby told him, authorized me to deduce—on un-suspected applications of capillarity and the properties of the luminous substance contained in the jade corbels on the public thoroughfares. It was a matter of an astonishing biological chemistry, pushed such to limits that, if the Dauphiné's physician can be believed, those instruments permitted the synthesis of the principal active cells of the human body.

In addition, as identical apparatus subsisted in the ruins of Rhâ-twa-tçi, the city of hospitals and invalids, he claimed that that fabrication of living substances must have been utilized in therapeutics, either for the purpose of grafting, or in other procedures.

To the astonishment that Toby and Jack Diver manifested one day before his enthusiastic affirmations, elevating that vanished people above the civilizations we know, while placing on a porcelain table-top a little casing of varnished sandstone, fitted inside with a delicate system of porous Lilliputian partitions and minuscule tubes, he replied:

"You ask how no echo of this science, no reflection of this extraordinary work, influenced the ancient world? But it's sufficient that this continent was isolated in the middle of the Atlantic, without neighbors, a universe sufficient to itself, as is proved, in any case, by the lack of means of artificial defense, the absence of any weapons, and the small dimension of its ships, not equipped for long crossings. Did not China, enclosed behinds its walls as these people doubtless were, realize a relatively refined and complex state of civilization in the epoch when Europe was inhabited by tribes living in almost absolute barbarity?"

"However," Toby remarked, "these people possessed a fleet. Now, it sometimes happens that a vessel is drawn by a tempest far from its route; we know something about that..."

"Well," the doctor replied, "I admit that one of their ships might have strayed toward the Iberian or Celtic shores. Supposing that its crew was not massacred, what influence could those castaways have exercised on a tiny tribe living on the coast, without any great communication with the interior?"

"That's true," said Jack Diver. "We're even able to take account of that, now I think of it. In fact, the Patagonians and the Fuegians, for example, certainly maintain more communication with present civilizations than ancient peoples probably had with the inhabitants of this land. Now, if a global cataclysm destroyed our continents today, only sparing Tierra del Fuego and Patagonia, do you think that future centuries would discover, in the oral or written traditions of those savages, traces of our science and our institutions sensibly different from those that Atlantis has left of its own in the Greek and Roman manuscripts that have reached us?"

"Furthermore," Toby added, "it seems to me that we're already far from being able to comprehend our own compatriots very well..."

Subsequently, he was obliged to observe the verity of that remark himself, since, a soon as he arrived in America aboard the *Hulda*, he was immediately interned in a lunatic asylum.

He was, therefore, right. For, whether one renders responsible a distant, mysterious prolongation of the physical influences that vanished race fashioned, or one attributes it solely to the effect of the multiple emotions successively felt by the passengers of the *Dauphiné* during their struggle with the elements, then at the moment of their imprisonment in the archipelago, and finally on contact with the vestiges of a subtle civilization, a strange reaction had operated in those souls

To begin with, the confusion of senses, about which Commandant Laffite had conversed with Lieutenant Rogés, that mixture of attributes imposing a color on sounds, mingling caresses with nuances, conferring a music on odors, had probably provoked a corresponding modification in minds.

If one adds to that a mild, enervating temperature, a recrudescence of the perfume, such that it enveloped the entire ship with its effluvia, one could perhaps admit that having brought about the disappearance of the usual categories, the neat, rigorous classifications to which men and women are accustomed to have recourse in their conversations in talking about touch, vision, taste, those singular perceptions, combined with the action of the voluptuous odor, had, by the same token, led the passengers of the *Dauphiné* also to doubt the value of other categories, other classifications. One would then have less difficulty supposing that, having thus made a tabula rasa of former modes of judging and feeling, they would be orientated toward certainties opposed to the previous ones.

A phenomenon was produced that remains, in spite of everything, not easily explicable in its entirety, but which I shall compare willingly enough to that determined by a magnetic mass introduced into the vicinity of a compass. The needle of consciousness indicated a new north!

In talking about that, Robert Toby declared, according to Tricard:

"It's at this moment that I understand why primitive peoples were right to erect statues and temples to the *** and the ***."

At that point the traveler of the Maison Loupe, of Bordeaux, used, instead of the familiar African fetishes, terms too gross, in European language, to be reproduced integrally.

In reality, it was a matter—this, at least, is what I have retained from Vincent Tricard's confidence—of a sentiment absolutely unknown to us, and which we are unable to represent to ourselves, even approximately. To try to translate that inversion of usual mental polarization would lead to naming as duty, licit, good and just "a variety of amour, variable systematizations of desire, successive or simultaneous, never involving correlative jealousy"—which would, evidently, become contradictory, according to our ethics, since it would be entirely immoral, and suppose a special state of mind that we are perfectly incapable of realizing, because it would be necessary for that that tradition, cupidity, hatred and modesty as well as a host of other affective and intellectual crystallizations would become in our eyes forms empty of any possible materialization...

And yet, that sentiment existed out there, manifested with intensity!

On that subject, Vincent Tricard had told me, after Robert Toby, numerous anecdotes, curious from the psychological and social point of view. I deeply regret that it is not permissible for me to report them here. That would have been my primary intention as a conscientious historian, but it has seemed to me, on reflection, that many of the details of that government of "amour," or, more exactly, "a particular variety of desire" would risk appearing merely paradoxical, if not scabrous and unhealthy.

I know full well that to such a reproach, Toby would have replied, as he had already said to Vincent

Tricard, that it is, on the contrary, us who, for want of having been confronted by the city under the mountain, remain "filthy."

XVII. Tim-Tçi

Standing in one of the corbels of the last terrace, his hands resting on the sculpted rail of a balustrade where the play of fantastic animals with the heads of vultures was depicted in mosaics of translucent enamels inserted in rare metals, Robert Toby, turning his back to the monumental staircase cleaving the golden vault in order to lead to Tim-Tçi, contemplated the immense agglomeration of ruins and palaces that was spread out beneath the dome of yellow metal.

The jade corbels outlined, by virtue of the emission of their phosphorescent waves, the avenues, the streets, the crossroads and the squares, whose agate flagstones shone, like immobile and milky water lit by the moon.

As if coming from an invisible population of birds inhabiting the forests of edifices and the hedges of the walls separating the cities, multiple songs rose up incessantly, bring the illusion of life.

Toby detached the ash from his cigar with a curt flick and turned toward Hallet, who was sitting nearby, in a kind of throne, around the arms of which coiled yellow ivory serpents, darting eyes of emerald.

"Do you know, old man," he said, "that I'm wondering whether it might not be better if we were to stay forever in this happy land, and Europe, America, and all the ignominies of the two worlds were definitively swept from the surface of the globe—for at present, it will be damnably difficult for us to live out there. When I think about it, I feel nauseated."

And I, Bob," Hallet replied, "tell you that we're more damned every day, and that the least of our minutes here is worth an eternity of tortures for us. I'd like, on the contrary, to tear myself away from the enjoyments of this impious paradise, but there is in this city, and in the islands that surround it, a spell against which my dreads soften…and I can only complain about it in the rare moments during which that satanic charm isn't operative."

Toby shrugged his shoulders. He was about to reply to his comrade when joyful voices resounded.

"Ah, here they are!" someone exclaimed.

Santony and Lieutenant Rogés arrived, in the company of Jack Diver, La Pascalieri, Dora Bowl and the Slow sisters

"You've been well-informed," said La Pascalieri to Bob. "It's for this morning!"

"Yes," the chef engineer confirmed, "my men have been working up there for two hours, and I think they ought to have finished now."

"Truly!" said Toby. "And according to you, Monsieur Santony, it's..."

"A marvelous instrument taking the place between the organ and the phonograph, to such an extent that Edison's apparatus becomes nothing but the rudimentary and imperfect instrument that it is. Besides which, ours doesn't make use of sheets of tin, and it possesses a power and a clarity of emission..."

"A perfected barrel organ, then!"

"Not at all, for it's not the sounds of various instruments, more or less well imitated, but the perfect reproduction of complex music, accompanying human voices. Its location, underneath the central stage of the Polygonal Theater, seems to indicate that it was used to prevent the spectator from being distracted by the sight of massed choirs and the performers of the orchestra.

"The project of the performance is on, then, more than ever!"

"Certainly," replied La Pascalieri. "After the audition that Monsieur Santony is going to offer us shortly, Jack will reconstitute a work of which…we have the scenery and the costumes."

"What's this new story?" Toby interrogated.

"It's the truth," Jack Diver replied, in his turn. "Yesterday evening, we found a store-room adjacent to the theater, with all its contents in excellent condition. I assume that the situation of Tim-tçi protected it against the dust that has amassed in the other cities, and that the intensity of its perfumes has embalmed, in the double sense of the word, the fabrics of its villas and those of the garments we've discovered. Among the passengers, including the emigrants, it won't be difficult for us to recruit a sufficient backing cast. As for the leading roles, you know, don't you…?"

A formidable roaring, intercut with brief whistling sounds, interrupted her. Then there was a cascade of dull rumblings, which caused the enamel mosaics to tremble in their metal frames.

After a few seconds of communal anguish, a voice murmured timidly: "Don't all shut up like that!"

Dora Bowl, trembling, had taken La Pascalieri's hand, and, huddling against the singer, raised her wide and fearful eyes to the brown face, repeating: "It's necessary not to remain mute like this. Say something darling! Speak, I beg you!"

Toby attempted to joke: "Are those the chords of our instrument, already, Santony?"

But the engineering officer did not reply. He looked at Rogés, who turned his head.

La Pascalieri had seen them; she cried: "What is it, then? One would think that you know…come on, Philippe…what was that noise?"

Dora Bowl went on, softly: "Oh, tell me that we're not going to die…darling, darling, tell me!"

Miss Jane Slow smiled disdainfully at that emotion, and while her sister Marjorie tried to calm Dora down she declared, in a very calm tone: "Don't you remember, Marjorie, that after the Deluge, and the Ark miraculously saved, there was Sodom and Gomorrah, which constrained God to get angry again. Well, yes, Dora, we're going to pay the price for our happy life. For myself, I don't find it too dear. What about you, Messieurs?"

Rogés, Santony and Jack Diver dared not articulate a single word. Dora Bowl clung more tightly to La Pascalieri, who made the sign of the cross.

Hallet muttered: "It was bound to end like this."

"Come on, come on!" said Toby, violently. "Do you believe, then, that a tidal wave distinguishes between deserted beaches and criminal cities? That a catastrophe lingers over the choice of which humans to strike? Then again, if that noise came from an earthquake, we'd have felt the shock. It's doubtless a matter of the landslide of a rumbling cliff…perhaps also, cannon-shots of a ship in sight…how do we know whether the fog of recent days hasn't dissipated, allowing our watchmen to perceive a vessel, and appeal to it thus?"

"No, Monsieur Toby," said Miss Jane Slow. "What's the point in deceiving ourselves with futile hopes? It wasn't a signal by our watchmen, nor a signal from another vessel. It was the last plaint of our poor *Dauphiné*—whose boilers exploded—haven't they, Monsieur Santony?—when the anchor-chain, which didn't give way, this time—isn't that so, Lieutenant?—

dragged it under water just now, where the entire archipelago is following it at this moment..."

"It's frightful," cried Jack Diver, "what you're imagining there!"

"I'm not imagining anything," she went on, calmly. "Look!" She went to the balustrade, and pointed at the three cities. "Look! The sea is rushing to the conquest of that city, which defied it for such a long time...the lights are going dark...and the water's rising, carrying away the phosphorescent soul of the jade corbels...it's rising, almost soundlessly, with little giggles and kisses...rejoicing in finally possessing the city... Look, it's reaching the first terrace..."

"Enough, Jane! Oh, for mercy's sake shut up!" Marjorie implored.

Dora Bowl was sobbing. La Pascalieri, listening to her weeping, advanced toward Santony, Rogés and Jack Diver.

"So it's true, and you're listening to all that without budging, you...men! No, you   !"

She stung them with a base insult proffered in her native tongue; then, abruptly separating herself from Dora Bowl, who fell to her knees. She ran down the stairs, wild and alone, toward the waves whose white drool was now soiling the onyx of the steps leading to the second terrace

Rogés, surprised at first by the rapidity of that action, then launched himself after the singer.

"Lina! Lina!" he shouted. "Where are you going? It's absurd! Stay with us! Here, we're still safe for some time, and this accursed flood might stop...diminish...as it did the other evening... Lina!"

She did not even turn round.

He raced down the steps in his turn, and then both of them disappeared around a corner on the landing.

No one thought of going after them.

Hallet had sat down again in the throne around whose arms the ivory yellow serpents coiled, darting their emerged eyes, and looked at Dora Bowl with a bewildered expression, who continued weeping.

Toby chewed his extinct cigar.

Santony was talking in a low voice to Jack Diver and the Slow sisters.

Suddenly, a cry rang out, and a few moments later, they saw the lieutenant running precipitately.

"Come!" he said, with grand gestures. "Come on, all of you! A boat! Our boat, waiting at the quay! They're looking for us!"

A new appeal struck the vault.

Rogés replied: "This way, lads, this way!"

Soon, they made out the rhythmic sound of oars, and, surrounded by phosphorescent globules carried by the waves, a boat steered toward the stairway.

In the little group presently united, a feverish and joyful animation had replaced the stupor and desolation of a moment before.

La Pascalieri explained: "It's me they perceived! I knew that it was necessary to do something! If I'd obeyed you, well, we certainly wouldn't have seen anything…or heard the sailors hailing us…"

As the boat approached, an admirable music began to descend from the golden vault. Imposing and grave, and tender and passionate, with unknown sonorities and notes of a strange timbre, a powerful harmony mingled its fanfares and choruses with the delicate melodies of singular instruments.

"The organ! The organ of Tim-Tçi!" groaned Santony. "And my men up there, who have no suspicion..."

The boat touched ground.

A crew-master got out, and, touching his beret, said: "The *Dauphiné* has blown up. And we nearly went down with her, at that moment...the sea's still rising! It's necessary to embark quickly; otherwise...we'll no longer be able to get out!" He pointed to the great arch under which the monuments of Fu-twa-tçi were cut out in silhouette, surmounted by a strip of gray sky; the sea was reaching the frontons and the domes.

The women took their places in the boat, and then the men.

When Santony's turn came, the chief engineer said to Rogés: "Go! I'm staying."

"I'll stay with you," said the lieutenant.

"No! Your duty is to go. Anyway I should have died out there, on board, with our officers. They kept the fires lit in order not to risk, as long as the coal lasted, missing a possible opportunity of deliverance. I should have been out there just now. Go! Don't compromise your last chance of salvation! I can't ask you to wait while I go to look for my poor mechanics...you can't wait...you mustn't wait. Hurry, Rogés!"

The lieutenant hesitated.

"We don't want, either, in these conditions...," said Toby and Jack Diver. "Let someone climb up to Tim-tçi...and..."

A gesture from Santony stopped them. His voice became hard to say: "No childishness! You can imagine that it's not with a light heart that I'll sacrifice my men. At least let the sacrifice serve for something! I'm the oldest officer here; Lieutenant Rogés, I order you to go!"

Rogés embraced him, weeping, and obeyed. Up above, the symphony continued its moving song, whose chords dominated the splashing of the waves. Santony went up toward it, after having seen the boat draw away.

Heavily laden, it only advanced very slowly, in spite of Toby and Jack Diver having taken oars to aid the four oarsmen of the crew. An intense current, proving that the sea was continuing to rise, opposed their progress, which was also hampered by various pieces of wreckage colliding with the prow and the hull. They were continually caught up in the floating barrages formed by the multiple debris. Abrupt waves struck the bow. It took them an hour to get as far as Fu-twa-tçi, when the distance could normally be covered on foot in less than twenty minutes. Then, new difficulties emerged: the highest and most solid edifices had been transformed into reefs, and the keel often scraped the roof of a palace...

Finally, when they had crossed that dangerous passage and found themselves close to the enormous arch that opened to the sea, Rogés could not retain a cry of rage.

The men ceased rowing, and while the crew-master retained the boat by hooking it on to a nearby dome with his gaff, they all looked...

Under a low sky, where heavy black clouds were racing, through the oblique shafts of a dense rainfall, they perceived, rushing to assault the grotto, at the entrance of which the roofs of the monuments of the façade retained them, the flotilla of long Atlantean ships, set adrift, grouped there by the current, shaken at random by giant waves that threw them against one another noisily.

Like a crazed flock of black rams, ardent to fight one another, they raised their impatient prows on the crests of the waves, impatient to hurl themselves at one another in repeated impacts, in which their flanks were ripped and their masts fell, groaning, entangling their rigging, covering the waves with wrecks. And behind their moving masses, the swell, whipped up by a tempestuous wind, sent forth glaucous squadrons helmed with foam, charging furiously to collapse thereafter, rear up again imperiously, and collapse again...

"It's impossible to get through that insensate tangle of hulls," Jack Diver whispered in Toby's ear. "In any case, even without it, our boat couldn't get very far in that unchained ocean. Fate is definitely against us!"

"Bah!" Toby replied. "If we can succeed in holding firm for a while, those diabolical boats will end up being reduced to matchwood, and will no longer constitute an obstacle. As for the sea, it will calm down too..."

"You're mad, Bob," said Hallet, then, who had heard. "It's punishment, and we won't escape it!"

As if to corroborate Hallet's words, a terrible whirlpool caused the boat to spin. The crew-master nearly lost his balance, and let go of his gaff with an oath. Then, while a warm breath escaped from the grotto, fleeing over their heads, the passengers in the boat saw the last cupolas of Fu-twa-tçi swallowed up, and the great vessels in delirium advancing toward them...

Finally, a new undulation of the liquid mass threw the boat under the golden vault, definitively sealing the monumental arch, where the long black ships were crushed...

That happened so rapidly that only at the moment when the boat found itself separated by free space again, captive between the canopy of yellow metal illuminated by the reflections of the fluorescent waves and the sea strewn with incandescent globules, was there an outburst of cries aboard the little vessel, of noisy anger and despair, tears and imprecations...

Meanwhile, under the vast bell, the pressure of the air slowly increased as the mountain sank beneath the waves. It became more difficult to breathe. Roars filled the ears of the prisoners with a continuous clamor, and their eyes were blinded by a thousand darts springing from the polish of the gleaming plaques, trenchant flashes wrinkling the phosphorescent waters and the sharp glitter covering their garments, their faces and the rigging with a fulgurant network of sparks...

The sailors lay down on their benches. Hallet, kneeling down, was reciting prayers. Jack Diver, standing up, stiff against the mast, was mechanically whistling the tune of a negro dance, always the same, which he never finished, incessantly repeating the first four measures, cracking the knuckles of his entwined fingers. Toby, his benevolent face contracted by the chagrin of not being able to come to the aid of so much misfortune, sometimes looked at Rogés, who, conscious of having accomplished his duty, conserved a resigned attitude whose calmness was nevertheless belied by the nervous tics tugging at his face, and sometimes at La Pascalieri, caressing Dora Bowl and Marjorie, enlaced and moaning, with gestures of tenderness and consolation. Miss Jane Slow, her gaze absent, was smiling at memories or dreams...

The torture lasted for a long time—a very long time—in the fashion of a nightmare that one tries in vain to escape.

Gradually, all notion of the real abandoned those individuals thus tortured...

They arrived at no longer knowing whether they really existed, whether they had once counted among them people who had lived under the sun, and their past retreated into a distance such that they doubted having experienced it. They were not astonished that each of them took on, for his companions, the appearance of a phantom agitating feebly in a deafening and empty tumult, in a vain illumination, in a cruelly splendid décor...

There came a moment when their fatigued eyelids lowered and they abandoned themselves, very wearily, to the monotonous swell...

One of the mariners, hallucinated, doubtless believing that it was a candlelit evening, started to sing, gravely:

> *The moon on the waters.*
> *Without needle or thimble, thread or scissors*
> *Has woven for my beauty*
> *A veil of lace*
> *So fine and so thin,*
> *So beautiful and well made that the king desired her...*

Then a nearby voice responded, waking the sailors and the passengers with a start of astonishment:

> *So fine and so thin,*
> *So beautiful and well made that the king desired her,*
> *And he said to me, "Jean-Pierre,*
> *I'll send you to the galleys*
> *If you don't go in quest*
> *Over the sea, in this pretty sailboat...*

"Ahoy the boat!"

The specters became human beings again. Someone shouted: "Ahoy! Hope! Who are you?"

It was one of Santony's mechanics, left on watch to monitor the progress of the inundation near the monumental staircase leading to Tim-tçi, toward which the boat had come back.

At present the sea almost filled the immense grotto that had sheltered the three cities. Only the fourth still remained intact.

Soon, Santony, alerted by the man, appeared himself and, informed by Rogés, told him to put all his personnel ashore. He was occupied in tunneling through a place that he thought to be of limited thickness, sure that that part of Tim-tçi must correspond to one of the steps that the passengers of the launch had perceived a month earlier. Thus, with the precious reinforcement of the lieutenant's sailors, with a few blows of the pick-ax, they might perhaps be able to obtain an opening sufficient for the boat to be brought to the flank of the mountain, for he preferred it to the raft that he had hastened to improvise.

It was still permissible to hope, he affirmed, for the movement of the land's descent, still remained very slow, and did not oppose the realization of his plan. If the engulfment were retarded, or suspended, for only a few hours, the probability of salvation would be transformed into a certainty.

They listened to him without enthusiasm.

Nevertheless, they all disembarked.

One man remained on watch next to the boat.

XVIII. Air and Water

When the golden vault was crossed, the perfumes of Tim-Tçi, its splendors, and the joyful song of its hieroglyphs, restored some courage to the most despairing as soon as they had reached the portal guarded by gigantic elephants of red jade, with caparisons studded with gems, and they perceived the first houses of the city of pleasure, the only one that possessed private dwellings.

In the streets, carpets with faded hues replaced the agate flagstones of the other cities.

Its partitions of painted silk formed mobile, supple hedges, variously tinted, where baldaquins and soft door-curtains succeeded one another, with brilliant gaps enlivened by the mysterious phosphorescences that, in Tim-Tçi, redoubled their glare, for the walls of the grotto were coated with an unknown substance, with the consequence that Tim-tçi seemed to be constructed in the light of an immense opal, with fluid materials where the slightest flutter animated the images decorating the delicate facades with a singular and voluptuous light.

They reproduced, not without artistry, the various forms by which the agreeable, tender, violent, timid and audacious emotions were materialized. Alongside frescoes immobilizing dancers crowned with flowers, mimes and mummers, specifying their games, fixing their characteristic attitudes, medallions and panels did not hesitate to reproduce in their bold colors the troubling fury of sexual intercourse.

A population of passionate and joyful figures inhabited the double wall of shiny fabrics, which sometimes parted, as the garments of an immodest woman are disturbed.

The vestibule of a villa appeared then, showing the wooden steps leading to the apartments; and the mauve, pink, jonquil, blue or myrrh vision of its frail walls were completed by the lascivious gestures of its statues, a flash emitted by some mirror, or the fugitive magnification of reflections on the paunch of a metal vase.

Elsewhere, rents allowed the gaze to introduce itself into the intimacy of rooms, some in the form of shells, presenting in their recesses amphoras, cups and familiar objects, others of a more capricious configuration, designed for the convenience of enlacements. Some, bare, were only furnished with cushions, some of which still retained the indentations of the bodies that had made use of them. The majority were ornamented with a luxury of chairs, and tables on which crockery was displayed alongside forgotten bottles, become reminiscent of monstrous, fabulously iridescent pearls.

From The Elephant Gate, Tim-tçi extended in a fan to the Theater Quarter, situated higher up, on a platform sustained by squat pillars, framing a series of bas-reliefs sculpted in a substance the color of indigo, veined with gold seams, somewhat reminiscent of lapis.

That terrace was reached by mans of broad ramps, which the little troop guided by Santony climbed.

Soon, the sound of pick-axes dominated the crystalline music of the city of pleasure, it chirping and its murmurs, and they discovered the chief engineer's workmen at the corner of a kind of alleyway. A large black shadow already stained the sparkling wall.

The sailors ripped metal bars from neighboring constructions and rushed to their comrades' sides. Baskets were improvised with squares of cloth, shovels with fragments of banquettes taken from the nearest theater, and Jack Diver, Hallet, Toby and the Misses Slow, the plaintive Dora and even La Pascalieri busied themselves clearing away the debris, under the direction of Lieutenant Rogés, while the cavity was hollowed out in accordance with Santony's plan.

Everyone worked ardently, without exchanging a word. The breach increased in depth. From time to time, someone relieved the man standing guard by the boat. The inundation remained stationary.

The hours went by, intercut with brief rest periods. Hope was reborn, timid and bitter, soiled by the memory of the frightful explosion previously heard, by the frightful vision of the engulfment of the Dauphiné and the annihilation of hundreds of lives of friends, individuals with whom they had been rubbing shoulders that morning. Dora thought about her brother William, Rogés about his comrades, Laffite, the pilot and crew-master Trédurec, Santony about his five officers, the stokers and coal-heavers that he all knew by name. Everyone bore, with the joy that the thought of soon seeing the blue sky, the sun and the open air again gave them, the mourning of those deaths, near or distant but too numerous and too recent.

Nevertheless, when the workers at the face, in the depths of the narrow tunnel, began to hear an indistinct rumbling in which they recognized the voice of waves breaking on the other side of the mountain, they informed their companions delightedly, and a frisson of pleasure animated the captives.

One after another, they wanted to hear.

When they had filed out, a mariner, picking up his lever again, was about to set to work, but Santony seized his arm abruptly.

"Stop!" he said.

"Why?" asked the other, nonplussed.

"On the contrary, we need to hurry," exclaimed Hallet, "in order to get out of here sooner!"

"No!" replied the old officer. "Not so fast…"

There was a moment of stupor. They gazed with suspicious and curious eyes at the stones and the gray sand, as if to perceive the dangerous unknown that they concealed.

"It's a matter of not compromising our escape by an imprudence," the chief engineer went on. "One maladroit blow of the pick splitting that partition might be the end of us! The air accumulated under these vaults is slowing the progress of the waters down below. As soon as it escapes, their level will rise, and in proportions that we can't determine. So, in addition to the fact that a sudden release would risk, if not killing us, at least occasioning serious accidents, its immediate effect would be to submerge part of Tim-tçi. What would become of the boat, our unique means of salvation, in that sudden flood?"

"That's true! That's true! They cried. "Let's go fetch the boat first!"

"Indeed," said Rogés. Once the boat is in proximity with the issue, a few precautions will suffice."

It did not take long to transport the boat.

However, a vague dread persisted, keeping the workers away from their tools again. Jack Diver increased it by specifying it; for, as Santony and Lieutenant Rogés were discussing practical means of carrying out a kind of sounding that would permit the atmosphere of the grotto to lower its pressure slowly, the American raised a further objection.

"Permit me to interrupt you," he said to the chief engineer, who was talking about the probable level of the water outside. "Have you thought about what will happen if, contrary to your opinion, the mountain has already descended completely into the Ocean? An opening in that wall, and our air will escape...without us!"

"What do you mean?" interrogated La Pascalieri, who was listening.

"I mean," he replied, "that we're in a kind of diving bell, which might presently be situated, in the fashion of a real apparatus of that sort, below the surface of the waves, and that in that case, at the slightest little hole drilled there, we'd be trapped like foxes in an earth, caught between the water and the wall—or even, if the wall gives way, between two liquid layers..."

"Oh, that death would be atrocious! No, not that, not that! Let's wait, let's wait!" said La Pascalieri, seized by the terror that the vision of an immediate danger produces.

That terror they all shared.

To the rumors with which the ground was palpitating, and which had comforted them a moment before, they now attributed a terrible and menacing meaning. They believed they could hear, behind the thin partition of gray sand, the rumbling of the ferocious sea. And was not the partition itself about to give way, to open up? They considered it anxiously, also looking sometimes in the direction of the noisy city, the silken city by way of which death would come.

Thus, when Rogés hazarded: "But waiting will probably transform Jack Diver's hypothesis into certainty...," La Pascalieri cried: "Let's wait anyway!" And other voices repeated with her: "To be sure! Let's wait! We have to wait!"

The Santony spoke. "Yes, it's better to wait. If Monsieur Diver is right, that wall won't take long to show traces of infiltration; if it remains dry, we'll know that it's been permitted to us, by an exceptional favor, to escape the fate of our unfortunate companions. Now, all of you get some rest, during the few hours that it will need. I'll stand watch!"

Hastily, Toby said to the old officer: "Will you permit me to stand watch with you?"

They remained alone beside the wall, vibrant with tremors from outside.

For a long time, Toby resisted sleep; then, gradually, his eyelids lowered, and even though he was standing up, leaning against the tunnel wall, he did not take long to fall asleep.

When he woke up, it was with a red mist before his eyes through which he could no longer see Santony. Furthermore, a persistent noise of bells was ringing dolorously in his ears. It seemed to him that he was inside a prison of bronze whose metal was being struck rhythmic blows by a battering ram. Each stroke resounded within him, shaking his skull and bruising his temples. Sharp burns extended in waves of flame through his curbed limbs. At each inspiration, his breast encountered an unusual resistance, as if lead hoops were circling it...

And the bells were still ringing!

He tried to walk, but he staggered and stumbled over a recumbent body. He knew that it was Santony, and at the same time, as he attempted to help him, as he bent over, he fell down in his turn.

What had happened, then?

He tried to call out, without succeeding in doing so. Then he wanted, at least to see where the others were. He turned his head. The boat was blocking the corridor completely; he only saw a dark mass that filled his vision. He remembered confusedly, however, that the storage locker had been opened, the food unwrapped, that he would doubtless find alcohol there.

He reached the bow, with an effort that exhausted him, and was obliged to rest, almost stifled, while the bells rang more terribly in precipitate strokes. Then, hanging on to the edge, he took a step, and then another, and distinguished a bottle…but when he had taken hold of it, he had to let it go immediately, for the solidly-embedded cork was too firm; he would have needed both hands and al his strength. He was obliged to hand on to the boat, and felt faint.

Large tears ran down his face, damp with sweat.

Suddenly, he perceived a soft whistling, to which he hardly paid any attention.

Then, gradually, it seemed to him that the vice gripping his temples, his throat and his lungs was loosened. The opacity of the red fog diminished; the bells rang less ferociously in his head. He stopped weeping.

A moment later, he succeeded in digging a finger into the neck of the bottle, of which he had not let go. The cork was withdrawn. He drank avidly, and the red mist suddenly dissipated; the bells had almost stopped ringing…

The whistling persisted, coming from the depths of the tunnel. He turned to look at the partition—he could see quite well now. It was still dry, and a narrow fissure had torn it.

Then he understood, and launched himself forward, desirous of communicating the good news to everyone.

Toby's companions were lying on the heaped-up rubble, strewn with fabrics ripped from the nearby edifices. They had suffered no less than him from the increase in pressure to which the air had been subjected, and the pernicious effects of which were now lessening, thanks to the crack that it had ended up provoking. Breathless still, they were agitating confusedly. Some, on hearing Toby's footsteps, raised their heads, others propped themselves up on their elbows. All of them directed anxious gazes toward him.

Joyfully, he howled: "Saved! We're saved! No water! There are no traces of water! A crack's been produced. An escape that's whistling! So there's no water outside! Saved! This time, eh, there's no doubt! We're saved!"

Saved? They didn't seem to understand immediately. Then the word ran from mouth to mouth.

"Saved…!"

"Saved…!"

Sighs were exhaled. Joyful cries rang out.

They were breathing with increasing ease.

After having mopped his brow, Toby put his handkerchief back in his pocket, and found a cigar, which he lit delightedly.

The smoke designed spirals that fled toward the tunnel.

Everyone got up. The majority were tottering. Mariners were dancing. La Pascalieri was singing…

But the reaction soon changed. The perfumes of Tim-tçi, whose charm had been held in check in those men and women by the anguish of the preceding hours, the perfumes filling the silken city with an atmosphere of desire, recovered their power of lust.

A sudden folly transformed the recent despairs into ardent sensual intoxications. The fatalistic and Biblical stoicism of Miss Jane Slow, Hallet's fear, Dora Bowl's panic and sadness, Lieutenant Rogés' spirit of discipline,

La Pascalieri's fury, Marjorie's pity, the habits of respect and obedience of the workers and the mariners, amalgamated in the same delirium, in which they disappeared, absorbed by the sentiment about which we have all talked and which no one can either comprehend or describe...

Lips sought one another, hands joined.

In an instant, the alleyway encumbered by stones and its encampment of one night were deserted. The hiding place where they had awaited death was abandoned, in order to rediscover, before the liberating departure, sparkling Tim-Tçi, Tim-tçi and its floating essences, Tim-tçi and its villas of painted fabric, and its lascivious statues!

Perhaps also, at the moment of quitting their splendid life, they wanted to enjoy it one last time, to saturate themselves with the complete and subtle sensations of the land they were about to lose.

A communal frenzy carried them away.

Toby heard their kisses and their laughter drawing away as the course of the enlaced couples led them toward the terrace with the lapis bas-relief, from which one descended toward the city...

Why had he not followed them?

He judged himself stupid for remaining alone...

Alone...no! He remembered Santony, and went into the excavation.

He cocked an ear. The air escaping slowly through the fissure continued to sound softly at the end of the tunnel. He could not hear anything else.

Going past the boat, he reached the place where the chief engineer lay. He knelt down next to him, unbuttoned his jacket. It seemed to him that it was stained with patches of blood. He was trying to raise the old officer's head, carefully, when a violent shock threw him against Santony, in the midst of a deluge of sand, stones and a frightful tumult, which he scarcely heard, because he lost consciousness...

When Toby recovered consciousness, a light drizzle was moistening his face and hands. With stupefaction, he saw the sky overhead, and then, to one side, Santony's cadaver, his face wan, his mouth bloody, and, not far away the boat, which, half lifted up in the air, was swaying irregularly, gracelessly, jerkily, as if invisible had were weighing upon it at the rear. On the other side, the fleecy sea, a gray and white see, not too malevolent, whose waves were unfurling less than two meters away.

He got up painfully, his loins hurting and his back bruised, and he felt his limbs.

Definitely not: he had no other wounds than insignificant scratches; he had emerged safe and sound from that new adventure. A volley of spray that lashed his face, at the same time as an audacious wave came to drown his feet and submerge the body of the old officer, reminded him nevertheless that the situation remained precarious.

In very little time, in fact, he realized that the waters were still rising.

In the tunnel, those of the cavern were there, playing with the boat, scattering its oars, causing a frantic shaking, accompanied by an incessant racket. They were overflowing as far as the breach, into the narrow strip of ground on which Toby was standing, at risk of being carried away at any moment. It was therefore a matter of taking possession of the boat without delay.

But the prow continued its gymnastics. Toby tried to seize it, to draw it toward him, to drag it over the thin strand, but he only succeeded in bloodying his hands. It was necessary for him to penetrate into the corridor, to soak himself to the shoulders, in order to get to the stern of the boat. Afterwards, profiting from an eddy, he was fortunate enough to shove it vigorously, in such a fashion that the keel slid lightly, and this time, the prow found the wave.

Toby climbed on board and began to empty the boat with a scoop that he took out of a locker that had remained shut.

Suddenly, he fell on to a bench. After a second shock, he perceived that the boat, lifted by a wave, had quit the platform, now reduced to a minuscule tongue of mud, constantly swept by the waves, and that he was drifting away, for he observed that no trace remained of oars and equipment.

The current, however, drew the vessel away.

At one moment, Santony's body disappeared beneath the waves.

Then a short time afterwards, as Bob, simultaneously glad to be fleeing toward the sea, and saddened by that burial of the chief engineer, thought, with melancholy, about the *Dauphiné*, the happy life in the archipelago, his companions, their recent hopes, a seething of foam balanced the orifice of the tunnel.

Toby, having gone utterly pale, began to tremble miserably. His body was shaken by sobs. He fell to his knees, lowered his head, and wept...

In a cluster of cadavers vomited by the beach, spurting forth with shreds of fabric, lamentable and multiple pieces of wreckage, he had just recognized the convulsed face of Hallet, and, in the midst of interlaced nudities, the supple body of La Pascalieri, her brown face, the admirable oval of which had not been deformed by death, her mouth with the lips drawn back over excessively brilliant teeth, her eyes still laughing, her curly hair scattered and floating...

Honolulu August 1900-Paris November 1902.

SF & FANTASY

Adolphe Alhaiza. *Cybele*
Alphonse Allais. *The Adventures of Captain Cap*
Henri Allorge. *The Great Cataclysm*
Guy d'Armen. *Doc Ardan: The City of Gold and Lepers; The Troglodytes of Mount Everest/The Giants of Black Lake*
G.-J. Arnaud. *The Ice Company*
André Arnyvelde. *The Ark; The Mutilated Bacchus*
Charles Asselineau. *The Double Life*
Henri Austruy. *The Eupantophone; The Olotelepan; The Petitpaon Era*
Barillet-Lagargousse. *The Final War*
Cyprien Bérard. *The Vampire Lord Ruthwen*
S. Henry Berthoud. *Martyrs of Science*
Aloysius Bertrand. *Gaspard de la Nuit*
Richard Bessière. *The Gardens of the Apocalypse; The Masters of Silence*
Chevalier de Béthune. *The World of Mercury*
Albert Bleunard. *Ever Smaller*
Félix Bodin. *The Novel of the Future*
Pierre Boitard. *Journey to the Sun*
Louis Boussenard. *Monsieur Synthesis*
Alphonse Brown. *City of Glass; The Conquest of the Air*
Émile Calvet. *In a Thousand Years*
André Caroff. *The Terror of Madame Atomos; Miss Atomos; The Return of Madame Atomos; The Mistake of Madame Atomos; The Monsters of Madame Atomos; The Revenge of Madame Atomos; The Resurrection of Madame Atomos; The Mark of Madame Atomos; The Spheres of Madame Atomos; The Wrath of Madame Atomos* (w/M. & Sylvie Stéphan)
Félicien Champsaur. *Homo-Deus; The Human Arrow; Nora, The Ape-Woman; Ouha, King of the Apes; Pharaoh's Wife*
Didier de Chousy. *Ignis*
Jules Clarétie. *Obsession*
Jacques Collin de Plancy. *Voyage to the Center of the Earth*

Michel Corday. *The Eternal Flame; The Lynx* (w/André Couvreur)

André Couvreur. *Caresco, Superman; The Exploits of Professor Tornada* (3 vols.); *The Necessary Evil*

Camille Debans. *The Misfortunes of John Bull*

Captain Danrit. *Undersea Odyssey*

C. I. Defontenay. *Star (Psi Cassiopeia)*

Charles Derennes. *The People of the Pole*

Georges Dodds (anthologist). *The Missing Link*

Charles Dodeman. *The Silent Bomb*

Harry Dickson. *The Heir of Dracula; Harry Dickson vs. The Spider*

Jules Dornay. *Lord Ruthven Begins*

Alfred Driou. *The Adventures of a Parisian Aeronaut*

Odette Dulac. *The War of the Sexes*

Alexandre Dumas. *The Return of Lord Ruthven*

Renée Dunan. *Baal; The Ultimate Pleasure*

J.-C. Dunyach. *The Night Orchid; The Thieves of Silence*

Henri Duvernois. *The Man Who Found Himself*

Achille Eyraud. *Voyage to Venus*

Henri Falk. *The Age of Lead*

Paul Féval. *Anne of the Isles; Knightshade; Revenants; Vampire City; The Vampire Countess; The Wandering Jew's Daughter*

Paul Féval, *fils. Felifax, the Tiger-Man*

Charles de Fieux. *Lamékis*

Fernand Fleuret. *Jim Click*

Louis Forest. *Someone is Stealing Children in Paris*

Arnould Galopin. *Doctor Omega*; *Doctor Omega and the Shadowmen* (anthology)

Judith Gautier. *Isoline and the Serpent-Flower*

H. Gayar. *The Marvelous Adventures of Serge Myrandhal on Mars*

Louis Geoffroy. *Apocryphal Napoleon*

G.L. Gick. *Harry Dickson and the Werewolf of Rutherford Grange*

Raoul Gineste. *The Second Life of Doctor Albin*

Delphine de Girardin. *Balzac's Cane*
Léon Gozlan. *The Vampire of the Val-de-Grâce*
Jules Gros. *The Fossil Man*
Jimmy Guieu. *The Polarian-Denebian War* (2 vols.)
Edmond Haraucourt. *Daah, the First Human; Illusions of Immortality*
Nathalie Henneberg. *The Green Gods*
Eugène Hennebert. *The Enchanted City*
Jules Hoche. *The Maker of Men and His Formula*
V. Hugo, P. Foucher & P. Meurice. *The Hunchback of Notre-Dame*
Romain d'Huissier. *Hexagon: Dark Matter*
Jules Janin. *The Magnetized Corpse*
Michel Jeury. *Chronolysis*
Gustave Kahn. *The Tale of Gold and Silence*
Gérard Klein. *The Mote in Time's Eye*
Fernand Kolney. *Love in 5000 Years*
Paul Lacroix. *Danse Macabre*
Louis-Guillaume de La Follie. *The Unpretentious Philosopher*
Jean de La Hire. *The Fiery Wheel; Enter the Nyctalope; The Nyctalope on Mars; The Nyctalope vs. Lucifer; The Nyctalope Steps In; Night of the Nyctalope; Return of the Nyctalope*
Etienne-Léon de Lamothe-Langon. *The Virgin Vampire*
André Laurie. *Spiridon*
Gabriel de Lautrec. *The Vengeance of the Oval Portrait*
Alain le Drimeur. *The Future City*
Georges Le Faure & Henri de Graffigny. *The Extraordinary Adventures of a Russian Scientist Across the Solar System* (2 vols.)
Gustave Le Rouge. *The Dominion of the World* (w/Gustave Guitton) (4 vols.); *The Mysterious Doctor Cornelius* (3 vols.); *The Vampires of Mars*
Jules Lermina. *The Battle of Strasbourg; Mysteryville; Panic in Paris; The Secret of Zippelius; To-Ho and the Gold Destroyers*
André Lichtenberger. *The Centaurs; The Children of the Crab*
Maurice Limat. *Mephista*

Listonai. *The Philosophical Voyager*
Jean-Marc & Randy Lofficier. *Edgar Allan Poe on Mars; The Katrina Protocol; Pacifica 1, 2; Robonocchio; Return of the Nyctalope;* (anthologists) *Tales of the Shadowmen 1-12; The Vampire Almanac* (2 vols.)
Ch. Lomon & P.-B. Gheuzi. *The Last Days of Atlantis*
Camille Mauclair. *The Virgin Orient*
Xavier Mauméjean. *The League of Heroes*
Joseph Méry. *The Tower of Destiny*
Hippolyte Mettais. *Paris Before the Deluge; The Year 5865*
Louise Michel. *The Human Microbes; The New World*
Tony Moilin. *Paris in the Year 2000*
José Moselli. *Illa's End*
John-Antoine Nau. *Enemy Force*
Marie Nizet. *Captain Vampire*
Charles Nodier. *Trilby and The Crumb Fairy*
C. Nodier, A. Beraud & Toussaint-Merle. *Frankenstein*
Henri de Parville. *An Inhabitant of the Planet Mars*
Gaston de Pawlowski. *Journey to the Land of the 4th Dimension*
Georges Pellerin. *The World in 2000 Years*
Ernest Pérochon. *The Frenetic People*
Pierre Pelot. *The Child Who Walked on the Sky*
Jean Petithuguenin. *An International Mission to the Moon*
J. Polidori, C. Nodier, E. Scribe. *Lord Ruthven the Vampire*
P.-A. Ponson du Terrail. *The Immortal Woman; The Vampire and the Devil's Son*
Georges Price. *The Missing Men of the* Sirius
René Pujol. *The Chimerical Quest*
Edgar Quinet. *Ahasuerus; The Enchanter Merlin*
Henri de Régnier. *A Surfeit of Mirrors*
Maurice Renard. *The Blue Peril; Doctor Lerne; The Doctored Man; A Man Among the Microbes; The Master of Light*
Restif de la Bretonne. *The Discovery of the Austral Continent by a Flying Man; Posthumous Correspondence* (3 vols.)
Jean Richepin. *The Crazy Corner; The Wing*

Albert Robida. *The Adventures of Saturnin Farandoul; Chalet in the Sky; The Clock of the Centuries; The Electric Life; The Engineer Von Satanas*

J.-H. Rosny Aîné. *Helgvor of the Blue River; The Givreuse Enigma; The Mysterious Force; The Navigators of Space; Vamireh; The World of the Variants; The Young Vampire*

Marcel Rouff. *Journey to the Inverted World*

Marie-Anne de Roumier-Robert. *The Voyage of Lord Seaton to the Seven Planets*

Léonie Rouzade. *The World Turned Upside Down*

Han Ryner. *The Human Ant; The Superhumans*

Louis-Claude de Saint-Martin. *The Crocodile*

Frank Schildiner. *The Quest of Frankenstein*

Pierre de Selenes: *An Unknown World*

Norbert Sevestre. *Sâr Dubnotal: Vs. Jack the Ripper; The Astral Trail*

Angelo de Sorr. *The Vampires of London*

Brian Stableford. *The Empire of the Necromancers (1. The Shadow of Frankenstein; 2. Frankenstein and the Vampire Countess; 3. Frankenstein in London); Eurydice's Lament; The New Faust at the Tragicomique; Sherlock Holmes and The Vampires of Eternity; The Stones of Camelot; The Wayward Muse.* (anthologist) *News from the Moon; The Germans on Venus; The Supreme Progress; The World Above the World; Nemoville; Investigations of the Future; The Conqueror of Death; The Revolt of the Machines; The Man With the Blue Face; The Aerial Valley; The New Moon; The Nickel Man; On the Brink of the World's End; The Mirror of Present Events; The Humanishere*

Jacques Spitz. *The Eye of Purgatory*

Kurt Steiner. *Ortog*

Eugène Thébault. *Radio-Terror*

C.-F. Tiphaigne de La Roche. *Amilec*

Simon Tyssot de Patot. *The Strange Voyages of Jacques Massé and Pierre de Mésange*

Louis Ulbach. *Prince Bonifacio*

Théo Varlet. *The Castaways of Eros; The Golden Rock.; The Martian Epic* (w/Octave Joncquel); *Timeslip Troopers* (w/André Blandin); *The Xenobiotic Invasion*
Pierre Véron. *The Merchants of Health*
Paul Vibert. *The Mysterious Fluid*
Villiers de l'Isle-Adam. *The Scaffold; The Vampire Soul*
Gaston de Wailly. *The Murderer of the World*
Philippe Ward. *Artahe; Manhattan Ghost* (w/Mickael Laguerre); *The Song of Montségur* (w/Sylvie Miller)

Victor Margueritte. *The Bacheloress; The Companion; The Couple*

NON-FICTION

Stephen R. Bissette. *Blur 1-5. Green Mountain Cinema 1; Teen Angels*
Win Scott Eckert. *Crossovers* (2 vols.)
Georges Grison. *The Heads that Fell in Paris*
Jean-Marc & Randy Lofficier. *Shadowmen* (2 vols.)
Randy Lofficier. *Over Here*
Brian Stableford. *The Plurality of Imaginary Worlds*